Contents

CHAPTER ONE

The moon stood full and round in the naked sky. There were no clouds, no stars, not even trees to block it from view. Nokemono's eyes widened as she stared up at it. The mountains were silent at this time of night, but beneath the silent was the patient presence of things that watch in the dark. Nokemono gritted her teeth. She had made a companion of loneliness, but this felt *different*.

Hinadori had left her. That stung more than the thick bruises along her side, but she bore it with the same mindful indifference. Akari was gone, too. That was a deeper, more personal hurt.

Whenever she closed her eyes, she saw Akari's haunted face as the temple door closed on it. Over and over, she relived that unspeakable moment when Akari went to die. *It was my fault.*

She turned on to her back and felt a sharp slap of pain shoot up her side. She groaned and bunched up her fists. A lonely tear rolled down her cheek. Nokemono sucked in a breath and flicked it away. She heard the sudden sweep of leaves being brushed aside as something slithered in the bushes. She didn't care. Let it come. The worst had happened and fear was no competition for her dreams.

A sharp, shrill wind blew through her and Nokemono pulled her only cloak tighter about her arms. The night grew quiet and still as the witching hour came. She lay awake waiting, half-expecting for some creature of the night to bring death her way – but nothing came. Helpless as she was, it seemed even the mountain beasts thought she was best left alone.

When morning broke and the moon swapped places with the sun, she had barely gotten a wink of sleep. She got to her feet and stretched down until she heard a soft crack in her back. She brushed down her cloak and tilted her neck one way, then the other.

There is an energy that becomes available after a close call with death. Nokemono had slept alone, beneath the stars in a place that most wouldn't travel in the day. And here she still was. It was a confirmation and a clarification. *I am here for a reason.*

The night had done its worst. *I'm still here.*

She dropped to her knees and stared up at the sky, whispering her petition to the gods. "They took my father's blade. They have my only friend. The person who was the closest thing I have ever had to a parent is dead. One way or another, I will take everything back."

She straightened up and glanced over her shoulder. A stream led down the mountain, lined with a parade of trees. Somewhere down that way was a temple and in it was the thing

Noke knew she must have. She could still feel her hands tingling. The wondrous power.

They called it Kazeshini. The Wind of Death. A sword which demanded blood every time it was drawn from its sheathe. That blade had called out to her as clearly as anyone who had ever said her name. This was not something purely physical - it was a deep spiritual bond. Powerful and subvocal. Even now her fingers twitched with the eager hunger to be reunited with Kazeshini. She belonged to it and it to her. It was a truth as obvious and unrelenting as the changing of the season. If she knew nothing else in life, she knew she must have Kazeshini – it was her destiny.

She started walking and as she strode down; Noke set her mind to figuring out how she would convince the monks to give her the sword. She was no blade master, nor did she have the money to buy it. Her jaw tightened. She remembered something her old friend Sochi had once said: 'There are no friends on the street.' – she had learned that the hard way more than once. If the temple wouldn't give her the sword, she would have to take it. *But how?*

Black village gates appeared ahead, and Noke stopped to catch her breath. She was tired, hungry and broken in ways that didn't show, but she would not be caught looking like it when she arrived at the gates. She washed her hands in the stream, brushed down her clothes and combed through her hair with her hands till it looked half-way presentable.

As she approached the gates, a familiar figure stepped out from the bushes. He was tall as a tree and his left eye was covered with a dark patch. The golden medallion about his neck glistened in the sunlight, and the sword at this side was as good as a confirmation that he knew the work of violence.

He glanced down at her and narrowed his eyes. "You," he whispered.

Nokemono gave a small bow. She was no milk-wet little girl, but she knew enough to play the part when it called for it.

The watchman arched an eyebrow. "State your name and business," he said in a voice flecked with impatience.

Nokemono cleared her throat, remembering what Akari had said when they had last come to face this man. "I come in peace. My name is Nokemono. I wish to visit the temple."

The watchman gave her a studying look and gestured to her thick burlap sack. "Do you have any weapons in there?"

Nokemono nodded. "Yes, I do."

The watchman pointed to the floor and nodded. "Let me see them."

Noke frowned and shook open her burlap sack. Though her dagger was gone, she still had the weapons they had taken from the Jade gang. Knives and such enough to stock a village kitchen.

The watchman stared down at the collection and narrowed his eyes. "How old are you?"

She opened her mouth to speak, then hesitated. "What month are we in?"

The watchman snorted. "San-Gatsu."

Noke winced. Her birthday had come and gone – she had completely missed it. She rubbed her chin and sucked in a breath. "I'm fifteen," she said.

The watchman shook his head, looking at the stockpile of weapons. "Fifteen," he said with a hint of disbelief. He looked back up at her. "You may come, but you cannot take these weapons in."

Noke nodded her acceptance. "Alright."

The watchman gave her a long, studying look and stepped aside. "Welcome to Yoto."

Nokemono bowed as she walked past, then she glanced back at him. "May I ask your name?"

The watchman's eyes widened with a hint of surprise, then he remastered himself and straightened. "Umino," he said.

Nokemono nodded. "My name is Nokemono."

She swept past him and made her way into the village. Yoto was a small, sparse village and its great centerpiece was the temple. It wasn't the biggest thing in the village, but from its simple, elegant design, it was plain that it was the most important thing. Built from unfinished wood with a distinctive gabled roof with decorative logs across the façade – it made a powerful impression. It occurred to Noke then that the temple might have been the only reason a village was there at all. She looked around at the other village; all the usual signs of life were there. A gaggle of chickens; a young man leading a goat with a tree branch. But there were other peculiar things too. For one, almost all the villagers were men in their later years with the simple, bent-backed slouch of those who spent a great time in prayer. For another, there was no village square, no market, no drinking house. Nokemono bit down on her lip. *They are all monks.*

She came at last to the temple and knocked once against the wood-paneled door.

It slid easily open and a small balding man stood in the doorframe. As soon as his eyes met Nokemono, they narrowed into thin slits of irritation.

Noke stepped back out of pure instinct. On the streets, she had been smacked enough times by wary stall keepers to know when the hits were coming. Just a subtle shift of the leg or lift of the eyebrow was enough to tickle her senses and tell her body that someone close wanted to thump her. Seeing the monk's eyes, all her internal alarms began ringing, and she shifted out of striking distance.

The man frowned, and she knew she had been wise to move. He was disappointed he couldn't get to her easily.

He made a disgusted noise and spat. The gob of saliva flew true and hit the soil behind Noke.

"You?" he hissed. "You dare to come back here after what you did?"

Noke cleared her throat. It was the monk who had passed the sentence of Akari –whose sword had done the bloody business. His features were soft and thoughtful in one way, but his eyes were hard as flint. He was a warrior monk – make no mistake. Noke could see it in the way he moved, the way his grip flinched around his sword. The way his shoulders were pulled back and his weight evenly distributed, with his feet spaced apart. She knew his name too, Akari had said before she died – Tanto.

Noke steadied herself. She had practiced half a hundred times what she was going to say when she finally got to the temple, expecting this very sort of reception.

She let out a breath and bowed low, spreading her palms wide and bending until her forehead touched the floor. This was the highest form of prostrate greeting – something even the most witless village dullard would know. A gesture of surrender, submission and solicitation.

She glanced up at him. "I have been called many things in my life. Street rat, parasite, scavenger," she hesitated, "stupid *eta* girl." Her jaw tightened. "All of those things may have been true in some small way at one time or another."

The monk's frown deepened. "I quite agree."

Noke stifled a frown. "But even I, low as this, am not beyond forgiveness. Not too far gone from redemption."

The monk's eyes narrowed till she thought they were closed. Noke smiled. She had him.

"Even the wolf who howls at the moon can still be brought again to light," Noke said, "that is the work of the temple. To be a light in the darkness. A place of restoration. Of sanctuary. Of redemption."

The monk made a low, irritated sound in his throat.

Noke straightened. "Do you not agree?"

The monk's temple throbbed with coiled rage. "It is as you say."

Noke gave a small smile. "Then you agree also that you cannot bar my entry to the temple that you are duty bound to hear my petition."

The monk spoke through gritted teeth. "I agree."

Noke dropped to a knee. "Then here is my petition. I throw myself at the feet of the temple, asking that I may be accepted as an acolyte that I too may one day return to the light. That I too may one day be worthy of wielding the Wind of Death."

The monk arched an eyebrow at the last and leaned forward. "Did you say wield the Wind of Death?"

Noke drew in a breath and nodded. "Yes."

The monk hissed out a spattered breath and then threw his head back and laughed, holding his belly as his whole body shook with incredulous delight. All his fury seemed to seep out as he laughed.

Noke felt the color rise to her cheeks but did not let her face fall. She had expected an astonished reaction, but it was important she made her intention clear. If there were things that would stand in her way, she wanted to know now.

The monk let the laughter die out and noticed that Noke was not laughing along. He hesitated and leaned forward. "Gods above," he said, still coughing with mirth, "you were being serious?"

Noke replied with cold certainty. "Yes, I am. I wish to wield the Wind of Death. I believe it is my destiny."

That sent the monk into another fit of laughter, and it took a while before he regained his composure to speak. "I'll give you this girl. You have mountains for stones, coming here again. Half the monks in this temple still say we should have whipped you bloody before we let you go. An innocent woman was forced to bear the punishment that you earned. That was…"

"Unforgivable," Noke finished, lowering her gaze, "no one knows it more than me. But Akari's sacrifice will not to be in vain, it has to mean something. That is why I am here. To make something of myself. Something extraordinary."

The monk's smile faded. "And you believe that means to wield the Wind of Death? Why not some other more realistic task? Why must you go after the sword again?"

Nokemono straightened to her full height, meeting the monk's gaze. "That sword called out to me. I can feel its presence even now," she said, pointing directly to the room she knew it was kept. "Kazeshini is my destiny. I have never been surer of anything in my entire life."

The monk gave her a serious, questioning look. "Is that so?"

Nokemono nodded. "It is why I couldn't help but take it before. Why it felt so natural in my hands."

Tanto snorted derisively. "That sword is the oldest thing you have ever seen, girl. Made more stories than you would even care to imagine. It hasn't been wielded in over a hundred years. Not even by the best, most skilled monks that have come from this temple. Not one person has proven themselves worthy. What makes you think you have even the whisper of a chance?"

Noke's lips curled into a slow smile. "Call it the ignorance of a stupid eta girl."

CHAPTER TWO

The temple was far bigger than Noke had realized. It had several underground floors that surrounded a single tunneling staircase. Peering over the staircase balustrade, she surmised that the temple descended to no less than three levels. It was an incredible marvel of engineering that Noke would not have imagined possible if she hadn't seen it for herself.

"What is this place?" she asked Tanto, who led her down the stairs.

His lips curled into an almost feral grin. "You'll see soon enough."

They walked one floor down and Tanto slid a door aside to reveal three stone benches built into the floor. "Wait here," he said, pointing.

Noke arched an eyebrow as she slid onto the bench.

Tanto gave her a scrutinizing look. "If you move an inch from that bench, that'll be the end of you here."

Noke frowned. "I understand."

He nodded once and slid the door shut as he took his leave.

Left alone, Noke was struck by the peculiar patterns painted on the walls of the room. They oscillating lines and circles that seemed to have no real meaning she could understand. The longer she stared, the more she felt lulled into a state of thick unease. There was a presence in the room. Something palpable. Noke didn't feel alone.

She looked around again. There were no windows or doors, save for the sliding one that Tanto had left close. No one could see her and yet she felt watched.

The door eased slowly open and Tanto appeared in the frame. He stepped forward and only then did Noke notice the short, bent-backed elderly man who stepped in after him. The older man was completely bald and his eyes were the shallow dark of an evening before full night. He moved with hands clasped in conspiratorial intent and had thick markings of tattoos across the front of his hands in black ink. His eyes met Noke's and he smiled.

The sudden flare of teeth almost made Noke fall from her seat. It was such a sudden, unexpected move that only her clenched jaw stopped the yelp that had started in her stomach. The smile was far from being pleasant. It was an easy, white-toothed smile, but it didn't fit the man's face or match his eyes. While the eyes were dark with malice, the smile was full of mirth. Something about it made Noke's stomach turn sideways.

"Welcome," the man said, narrowing his eyes, "I am Kasa."

Noke drew in a breath and gave a polite nod that resolved itself in a bow. "Nokemono."

The old man nodded and smiled. "Tanto told that you want to wield the Wind of Death."

Noke nodded. "Eventually."

The old man gave that mirthless smile again. "Of all the people that have come here seeking to wield it — you are by far the strangest."

Noke smiled. "Should I take that as a compliment?"

Kasa shook his head. "No."

Noke's smile melted.

"Do you know what we do here?" Kasa asked, moving to sit beside Noke on the bench.

Noke raised her chin. "You are warrior monks," she said easily.

Kasa arched an eyebrow. "And what makes you say that?"

Noke glanced up at Tanto. "Look at his arms," she said, pointing. "That is pure muscle. If I hit him, it would sound like I hit a tree. I have seen enough in this life to know that you don't get arms like that from reading and praying all day."

Tanto narrowed his eyes and drew down his sleeve.

"Look at the way you sit," she said, gesturing to Kasa's feet. "Your back is straight; your feet are stretched about evenly. Thos hands of yours haven't rested once since you stepped inside. I am a market girl – I know when somebody can hit. You, sir, know a thing or two about hitting."

Kasa smiled and finally let his hands fall to rest. "Clever girl."

"I learn fast," Noke said. "I work hard, be an outstanding student. This I give you my word."

Tanto shook his head. "She's petulant. Impulsive. She doesn't listen, and she has thieving hands."

"All the more reasons why I need to be trained. What would become of me if I kept thieving?"

"None of our business," Tanto snapped.

"That's enough, Tanto," Kasa said, gesturing with a hand. He turned to Noke. "How old are you, girl?"

"Fifteen" she said easily.

"And how long have you been on the streets?"

Noke narrowed her eyes. "As far back as I can properly remember."

Kasa narrowed his eyes. "What do you know of fighting?"

Noke smiled. "A thing or two."

Kasa's jaw tightened as he rose to his feet. "Show me," he said, raising both hands.

Noke arched an eyebrow. "What? Right now?"

Kasa nodded, holding his palms up in the air. "I want you to touch my robe. Just a touch."

Noke gave the man a studying look, watching the way his robes shifted gently in the wind. "Just one touch."

Kasa nodded. "Yes."

Noke lowered her head as though considering the proposal, then she lunged forward, cat-like, with hands raised. The old man was ready. He took a single, perfect step left, moving out of place and slapped her back as she darted past. It was a movement so fluid and fast that it took Noke a moment to realize what had happened.

"Streetside trickery won't work here," Kasa said with a hard look. "Touch my robe," he said, holding his palms up.

Noke gritted her teeth and sprung up to her feet. She darted left in a feint. Kasa stepped expertly right. She smiled as she moved to double back on him, slapping her hand out to snatch at a piece of flailing robe. Kasa smiled as he took a simple step back.

Noke had thought she had him, but when her fist closed, she clutched at thin air. Undeterred, she jutted immediately forward. Kasa slapped her down with a force that had the feel of retribution. She hit the ground hard.

"Just one touch," he hissed.

He was taunting her.

"I'll give you one touch," Noke snarled.

She grabbed and she snatched and she pounced. She didn't even come close. He was too fast; too nimble; too perfect. After a minute of trying, she was out of breath, bent over, puffing like a fish.

"Too tired?" Kasa asked, still fresh as a daisy.

"No," Noke said, as she rose to her feet.

She went after him again, and this time he hit back. It was only with the flat of his palm and even then, with controlled force, but more than once he caught her flush and bruises would follow.

She licked a tooth that had come loose, tasting blood.

Kasa's stare was pitiless. "The longer this goes on, the more force I will use with you," he said.

"Do your worst," Noke said as she lunged for him again.

She missed and his hand jutted out to slap her. Now Noke had been slapped before. In her time on the streets, she had seen more slaps than the mosquitos. What Kasa had done was no ordinary slap. He hadn't drawn back; he hadn't stepped forward. Kasa had reached out to her; the way one might reach out to a lover and the slap had come with such sudden speed, she didn't realize she had been slapped until the stinging pain made her jerk back. For all she knew, the slap could have come from the gods; she had never witnessed such effortless power.

She touched her jaw, feeling the loose tooth rumble about her bloody mouth. It would only get worse from there. If Kasa had been taking it easy on her before, only pain lay ahead. The man was small, but powerfully built. His palm was like oak and his speed was the wind. If he decided he wanted to hurt her, things would get bloody.

But Noke was a street girl. Pain was as familiar to her as the morning sun. If pain was all that stood between her and Kazeshini, she could deal with that. She spat the tooth out and wiped the blood away. *Just one touch.*

She kicked out at Kasa's thigh. He lifted his leg and stamped down on her knee, making her over-extend and fall into a messy split.

"Give up before this gets dangerous for you, girl. I will not take it easy," Kasa snapped.

That only seemed to spur Noke on more. She didn't like the way he said the words 'give up'. The way he called her 'girl'. Frankly, she was good and tired of his mockery. It was plain he was ten times the fighter she was, but she would not be his figure of fun. *Not on my life.*

She went after him again. He struck her down with another thick handed slap. Her ears were ringing and her nose was bloody. For the first time, she saw the sense of not standing back up.

She bit down on her lip, bunching up her fists as she got back to her feet.

Tanto stared at her in disbelief, then looked at Kasa. "Kyoshi," he breathed, "she is just a stupid girl."

Kasa narrowed his eyes. "Then there is wisdom for her to learn," he said.

Noke narrowed her eyes. She knew how this would go. She stood no chance of touching Kasa's robe. Her stubbornness was still there, but the man would only keep striking her down until she couldn't get up again. He wanted to send her back humbled. Make it so she would give the whole thing up. There was no winning this. At least not in any sensible way.

So she did something reckless. Something foolish. Something only a person who had lost all good sense of self-preservation would do. *A stupid eta girl.*

She jumped forward with arms wide, offering him an irresistible target. If Kasa wanted to stop her from touching his robe, he would have to hit her with enough force to drive her back. At that distance, such a hit would be devastating. She would break bones at the very least; die at the very worst. In effect, she was making him decide – break me or you lose.

She saw Kasa's eyes widen as he realized he would have to hit her. He drew his hand back. She closed her eyes, gritted her teeth. In that moment, she was ready to face the worst. But the hit never came.

"A touch," Noke whispered, as she wrapped a hand around Kasa's robe.

She glanced up at him. His face was a picture of disgust. She had called his bluff. He gave a resigned breath and shrugged.

"You are mad," Tanto hissed. "He could have killed you."

Noke nodded. "I want you to know this. I won't be frightened away by the threat of pain. Of broken bones, of bloody bruises. Not even death. I came here for Kazeshini and I mean to have it. One way or another."

Tanto's eyes widened as though just seeing Noke for the first time, then he glanced at Kasa – almost as though to confirm that the old man was seeing the same thing.

"That was reckless," Kasa said. "On another day I would have hit you so hard, you'd struggle to walk again."

Noke shrugged.

"You think that is what will make me admit you into our Order? Recklessness?" Kasa added.

"Some might call it bravery," Noke said.

Kasa touched his chin. "Some." He turned to Tanto. "Find her a place to rest for the night. Tomorrow, we will bring her before the conclave and make our decision."

Tanto nodded.

She watched Kasa leave and followed Tanto to a small room with a bed mat and cloth pillow.

"I'll bring something to eat in about an hour. Rest here and in the morning, they will decide your fate," Tanto said.

Noke gave a low bow, still licking at the bloody hole where a tooth used to be. "Thank you."

Tanto frowned, snorted and left.

Noke closed her eyes and sucked in a deep breath.

Tanto was coming back in an hour. *One hour to steal Kazeshini.*

CHAPTER THREE

Tanto stared at the sword which hung from the wall. He sucked in a deep breath and shook his head. "I think it is a mistake."

"That is for the conclave to decide, Tanto," Kasa replied,

"To even parade her before the conclave is an abomination. She is a thief with no sense of control."

"Have you forgotten who you were when I found you Tanto?"

"That was different," Tanto said.

Kasa's eyes were sunken, but his shoulders were level and his stance was strong. An impressive man, by any measure. Calm as the morning breeze but possessed of the quiet strength of the mountain.

"Is it truly?" Kasa asked.

Tanto's shoulders hunched and all the lines of knotted muscle along his forearm tensed and tightened. "The girl is a mere thief."

Kasa gave a weary smile. "The gods do not presume to judge a man until the last of his days and yet you wish to condemn a girl before she is two and twenty."

"We put ourselves at risk. We put everyone at risk." Tanto hissed.

"I ask again if you remember who you were when we first met?"

Tango frowned. "I was a foolish boy. A thief. Reckless. A drunk."

"You had killed a man, I recall. A dangerous boy, if nothing else."

Tanto lowered his chin and narrowed his eyes.

Kasa touched his shoulder. "And yet, look what you have become."

"That is not the answer I was looking for," Tanto said. "I will not change my mind on it, teacher."

"I do not expect you to. That is why we have a conclave. That through the will of men, we might know the will of gods."

Tanto's shoulders slumped forward, and he gave a solemn nod. He glanced up at Kazeshini one last time and turned towards the door. "Tomorrow then."

Kasa nodded. "Tomorrow."

The two men walked shoulder to shoulder as they left the room.

A few moments after they had gone, Noke slid out from under the table. She was breathing hard and her clothes were almost sweat through. Waiting for them to leave had been an exercise in agony. It was a few heaves for air before she caught her breath and straightened up.

She glanced up at the wall. Kazeshini hung from it like some ominous totem. Even sheathed it carried the brilliance of a star. Something about it screamed out to Noke in a way she couldn't deny or forget if she lived to be a thousand.

She took a step towards it and stopped. *Kasa vouched for me.* Tanto's words resounded in her head – 'the girl is just a thief'.

Maybe he is right. Maybe I am just a thief. So what?

Her hand tightened into a fist. The way Tanto had spoken about her. With such easy finality. He thought he had the measure of her and judged that she wasn't worth a sentence of consideration. *The girl is just a thief.*

She tapped her foot impatiently, trapped between sense and insolence, feeling the anger build within. She gritted her teeth. Tanto's words were making her furious, and she knew why. It wasn't that his words were not true; it was the casual, insouciant way he said them. As though it was the most obvious thing in the world. He had known her for all of three idle hours and he had already taken her measure, judged her and dismissed her as a thief without merit. A person of whom nothing more could be expected beyond a thief.

She stamped her foot and bunched up her fists. *I am more than a bloody thief. More than all your other little monk boys. I'll show you all. Prove it so you all can see. That a little street girl can become better than you,*

Just like that, her decision was made. She wasn't going to steal the sword; she was going to earn it. Fair and square. Then she was going to rub all their bloody monk noses in it.

She looked up at the sword and narrowed her eyes. "I'll be back for you soon."

She turned towards the door, not daring to look back. Kazeshini seemed to pull at her soul with every step, but she refused to look its way. She knew if she looked back, she would change her mind.

"What are you doing here?" a voice came from behind.

Tanto stood in the doorway, his jaw taut with coiled rage. He looked for all the world like he wanted to draw his weapon. Noke stepped back with her arms raised in protest.

"Nothing," she snapped back.

"Liar!"

His voice was sharp and sudden as the crack of thunder and it hit Noke with the same wicked force. He closed the distance between them with one angry stride and snatched her up by the cloth around her neck.

"You wanted to steal the sword, didn't you?"

Noke opened her mouth to speak, but the words didn't come out quickly enough.

"Tell the truth, you lying thief!" he shouted.

Something about him calling her a thief again made her snap. It was all well and good being called a thief when you stole something, but not now. Not when for the first time in her life she had chosen not to take something she really, truly, deeply wanted.

"Get your hands off me," she hissed and struck him at the wrist.

It wasn't a hard strike, nor was it particularly accurate, but it seemed to take Tanto by surprise. His grip loosened and she jerked her cloth free of it.

"What's going on here?" another voice called.

It was Kasa. He spoke with a serene calm, but his voice still tolled like a bell at the call to prayer.

"I caught her trying to steal the sword." Tanto said.

"Now who's the liar?" Noke snapped.

Kasa met Noke's eyes and she froze. "Speak no lies child, tell it to me true."

Something about the man's eyes seemed to make her heartbeat slow all the way down. She knew in that moment that if she lied, he would know.

"I did come to steal the blade," she admitted.

"I knew it," Tanto snapped.

"But I changed my mind," Noke snarled. "I wasn't going to take it. I swear."

"She's lying," Tanto said.

"If I am lying, then tell me this: did I have the sword in my hands when you found me?"

Kasa glanced over his shoulder to Tanto. "Did she?"

He shook his head. "She did not."

"And was I facing the sword when you walked in?"

Tanto lowered his chin. "No."

"Then tell me, monk Tanto, if I came here to steal that sword, why would I be walking away from it when it was right there for the taking?"

Tanto's frown curled into a disgusted snarl, and he waved her away, folding his arms.

"I wasn't going to steal it. I swear."

Kasa lowered his eyes. "I believe you, my child."

Tanto's eyes widened. "Your child?"

Kasa raised a hand, silencing him. "You chose not to steal it in the end, and that is what matters but you have still committed an offence."

Tanto started smiling.

"To enter a room in the temple with the permission of a senior monk is an offence in this temple. Ignorance of that rule is no excuse. Tell me, Tanto, what is the punishment for this offence? As memory serves, you were guilty of it many times in your youth."

"Seven lashes against the back."

Kasa nodded. "Seven lashes it is, then. Tell me, child, will you take your punishment now, or will you wait until you are before the conclave?"

Noke raised an eyebrow. "I imagine it would not be a pleasant introduction to the conclave if my first order of business is to be whipped in front of them."

Kasa nodded. "There have been many introductions and I agree that would rank among the less impressive."

Noke stroked her chin. "But if I am to serve my punishment now, who will be doing the lashing?"

Tanto's slow smile was all the answer she could need.

"Tanto," Kasa confirmed. "He caught you carrying out the act."

Noke nodded. "And if I wait until tomorrow?"

"Then one of the conclave members will do the lashing."

"So, I find myself in a tough place. Tanto clearly hates me."

"I do not, hate you."

Noke shrugged. "Strongly dislike them."

Tanto made a gesture as though adjusting a weighing scale.

"So, I choose between being flogged by someone I hate, or risking sullying my reputation with people I've never met who decide my fate."

Kasa nodded. "That's about right."

Noke nodded and dropped to one knee. "Then I submit myself to you, monk Tanto. To serve my punishment. I know you think that I am far short of the character that you allow to be trained in this temple, but I am willing and hopeful that I can change your mind about me. Perhaps, if you flog me yourself, you will see the beginnings of my character."

Tanto's eyebrows rose in what could only be earnest surprise.

Kasa smiled an approving smile and nodded in agreement. "Well said. Well said."

Tanto's eyes hardened again, and he formed a thin line with his lips. "Let's do it then."

Noke followed them down to a small room with a long wooden bench at its center. At the far wall was a long wooden pole with hemp rope tied around the stump.

Tanto pointed to the corner of the room. "Pick your cane."

At the corner of the room was a wooden table with three instruments of violence. The first was a whip of dried white horsetail woven together in tight, thick knots. If Tanto used it, Noke saw that it would bruise but not bloody her. She winced at the thought of purple blue blotches on her skin in the days to come.

The next weapon was a thin rope whip, which made a snapping sound whenever it straightened. The whip, she knew, would almost certainly draw blood. With ten lashes, that whip would leave her with scars to last a lifetime.

The third weapon was a thick slab of burnished wood. The sort of thick plank that one might find in a carpenter's workshop or leftover after the work of house builders. Noke stared at it curiously. Only a brute would use a slab of wood to lash someone. It simply was not the sort of thing you beat people with. Not in any civilized place.

Noke narrowed her eyes and made a calculated decision. She raised the plank and handed it over to Kasa.

"I have made my choice."

Kasa smiled and nodded his affirmation. "Wisdom beyond your years."

Tanto stared down at the slab, frowning. With the other weapons, he could have lashed with no restraint. Beat her with the freedom to give his anger free reign. With those weapons, he didn't run the risk of killing her. With the slab of wood on the other hand, Tanto would need control. If he let his anger loose with the slab of wood, he would bludgeon her to death.

"Bind her hands, Kasa," Tanto said quietly.

Kasa obliged, tying her by one hand to the pole at the far corner of the room.

Noke's heart started to beat at a frantic pace. She glanced up at Tanto and saw nothing beyond the raw, shaking hate. Suddenly, it didn't seem quite so unlikely that Tanto wouldn't let his rage free and beat her to death with a stick.

"Remove your kimono," he said, holding the wood plank high.

She slipped the kimono off her shoulder, gritted her teeth and stared at the blank wall. This was it. Her punishment. She was ready.

She saw Tanto's shadow move and stifled a gasp. But the blow never came. Noke stood there for a moment, suspended in the strange silence.

Noke hissed out a breath. "What's taking you so long?"

There was only silence. She glanced over her shoulder at them and caught Kasa at the corner of her eye. His face was a mask of awe. Tanto too stood frozen with his eyes wide with shock.

They were looking at her back

For the first time since she had heard him speak, Kasa's voice trembled with concern. "Where did you get these markings on your back? Answer me truly, child."

Her tattoos. They were staring at her tattoos.

"I don't know," she answered honestly. "I've had these tattoos since before I can remember."

Kasa lowered his head and dropped to his knees, staring at the ceiling. "Gods above," he raised his chin, tears filling his eyes. "Gods above, be with us. Have mercy on us."

<u>CHAPTER FOUR</u>

Tanto swung his sword and it slashed through the hemp rope. Noke let out a breath, rotating her hands as the blood returned to her fingers.

Kasa looked as though he had seen a dead man walk free. "Wake the conclave."

Tanto gave a start. "Teacher, it is the middle of the night."

"Now," Kasa snarled.

Tanto bowed and scurried out of the room.

Kasa gave Noke a long, appraising look and gestured for her to sit. She crossed her legs and lowered herself to the floor as Kasa paced back and forth about the room.

"Tell me again, child. Where are you from?"

Noke cleared her throat and straightened. "A town down the mountain. Nagiso. I grew up in the market there."

"And before the market, where were you?"

Noke lowered her head. "I…I don't remember. The market was all I knew."

"Who took care of you? Who raised you?"

"Different people, market people. Some kind, some not so kind. They never cared for very long. Well, at least not until Akari."

Kasa's eyes widened at the mention of Akari's name. "Did she ever see your tattoos? Akari?"

Noke tried to think back to the first day she had met Akari. When she had tried to steal from her market stall. Akari had a way of seeing things. Sometimes, when she looked at you, it was as though she could see beneath the skin.

"I don't know," Noke answered honestly, "she might have seen them."

Kasa shook his head, muttering half to himself. "Akari, Akari. What have you done to the world?"

Just then, Tanto burst back into the room, breathing hard. His forehead had a line of sweat, but it was plain he was trying to contain himself.

"Teacher, the conclave is ready."

Kasa nodded. "We'll be right there."

Tanto bowed and left. "Yes, teacher."

Kasa rested a hand on Noke's shoulder, scanning the room as though to check for spirits. Then he gestured to the door with his chin. "Let's go."

They slid into the corridor, illuminated by hanging torches spread three strides apart. Noke had half a hundred questions to ask and managed it only a few paces before she burst out with her question.

"What do my tattoos mean?" she blurted.

Kasa gave her a sharp, studying look. It was the sort of look a veteran horse trader might give a young stallion when deciding if it's worth his money.

He pulled open a door to reveal another corridor. The ceiling was lower, the path was narrow, and it sloped down such that you had to take each step slowly to stop from stumbling forward.

"After you," he said, ushering her forward.

Noke took a reluctant step, feeling the sense of dread build up in her stomach.

As they walked, Kasa cleared his throat and narrowed his eyes. "In a time, long before now. The House of Blood was not divided. We were one blood."

Noke raised an eyebrow. "The House of Blood?"

Kasa let out an exasperated breath and blinked. "The Bushido Academy and this magnificent temple were once one united school. Matters of both the spiritual and the temporal were once all taught under one roof. It was called the House of Blood and it had two masters - the master spiritual and the master temporal."

Noke nodded her understanding. "What broke it apart?"

Kasa offered an insouciant shrug. "It is hard to say. Some would say it was the arrogance of two men. Others would say it was an act of the gods that caused them to quarrel. Some even say that the spiritual and temporal should never have joined together in the first place."

"What do you believe?"

"Power is the bedfellow of conflict. The pursuit of it is a slow-working poison. When two people act in the pursuit of power, soon they will begin to see one another as a threat and eventually, as enemies."

"So… the Masters fought?"

Kasa frowned. "It was not so simple as that. In those days, the House of Blood was a force to be reckoned with.

They worked in pursuit of the greater good and answered only to will and word of the gods. The House of Blood didn't get involved in politics until Haruto, son of Ren, became the Master Temporal and decided to do things differently.

Noke nodded. "I see."

"Haruto asked an important question – 'How can we serve the will of the gods when we play no part in the world and hold no influence in politics?'"

"What did the Master Spiritual say?"

"The old Master Spiritual gave a simple answer - 'The will of the gods is found through acceptance, not through discovery'. That is what we believe to this day. It is in moments of quiet reflection that you discover the truth, not in studying the affairs of humanity."

Noke sucked in a breath, somewhat confused by the statement.

"But Haruto was not satisfied with that answer," Kasa continued. "He believed that the House of Blood should take a more active role in its community. Protect the people. Clothe them. Feed them. Show the people what is right."

"That sounds like a good thing," Noke said.

Kasa nodded. "In some ways, it is. But what happens when right and wrong are not so clear? What happens when two people are fighting and each one has a righteous cause? Who decides then? No matter how much we learn, we are still human. When you set yourself as an authority on what is right, you are playing god. You must let each man find his own way to righteousness."

"So, the Master Temporal left with all his students?"

Kasa raised his chin. "It was not a clean thing. There were some students of the Master Temporal who remained here, just as there were some under the Master Spiritual, who left. What really broke the House of Blood was Akai. The

Master Spiritual's daughter. She left with Haruto. After that, there could be no reconciliation. No matter how much the Master Spiritual was begged, he would never treat with the Master Temporal."

"So, the monks are the descendants of the Master Spiritual and the samurai are the descendants of the Master Temporal?"

"I suppose you could put it that way."

Noke gave an irritated look. "What does all that have to do with my tattoos?"

Kasa blinked. "In the old House of Blood. Those who had completed the training under both Masters Spiritual and Temporal. They would tattoo the powerful truth that they have learned from the gods on the backs of their children."

"I thought you said the House of Blood was broken up long ago?"

Kasa nodded. "It was – but there are some, perhaps one in every five generations, who manages to complete their training under both Masters. We call them the One Blood. Your tattoos mean your father was one of the One Blood."

Noke narrowed her eyes and bit down on her tongue as her jaw tightened. "Or my mother," Noke said.

Kasa gave a reluctant smile. "I suppose that is true. It might be your mother."

Noke touched her chin. "So let me get this clear. While the samurai go out into the world to keep the law, the monks…do nothing?"

Kasa narrowed his eyes. "You are a clever girl, Nokemono, but do not let your cleverness be the ending of you."

Noke frowned, feeling a trickle of irritation curl at the back of her throat. "So, what do you do then? I've never heard of you doing anything but praying and sleeping."

"You know nothing of our way and I need not explain our importance to you."

Noke hissed in irritation. "If I am going to learn from you, then I ought to at least know what it is all for."

"That is for you to learn. Not for me to explain. If you do not wish to stay, our doors are not locked. You are no prisoner. Leave for all I care."

Noke frowned. She wasn't leaving without Kazeshini. She knew in every filament of bone that it was her destiny to hold it again. If it meant studying under them, so be it. They came at last to a large double-door with ring-pulls fashioned of burnished silver.

Noke looked up to Kasa. "I'm not leaving."

Kasa took hold of a ring-pull and heaved a door open. "The conclave will decide that."

Noke glanced inside and saw three figures seated around a half-moon table. The one at the center had the boyish, beardless look of a prince in a storybook. He was by far the youngest of the three, with hair dark as the full of night and rust-hued eyes with a dim trace of silver. He didn't look directly at Noke, but all the while, she could feel him watching her. More than once, she rubbed her arms, thinking there was some small insect crawling over them, but each time she found there was nothing.

The man next to him had the weathered, grandfatherly appearance that Noke had expected of the conclave. His thick, storm cloud gray hair fell over his hunched shoulders such that Noke could barely see his features, but his eyes were shockingly clear. He, too, didn't look directly at her.

Last amongst them was a man who seemed to be the midpoint in age between the other two. His shoulders and arms were thick with cords of muscle and his chin looked like it had been chiseled from stone with a kill sharp flint knife. One look was enough to know that this man could kill. It was there in his arms, in his eyes, in his countenance. Everything about him screamed danger and only stubborn pride stopped Noke from running from the room and putting day and night between herself and the temple.

An unusual trio and none of them were looking at her in the eye.

Only then did she realize what they were looking at. A painting hung from the wall just to the left. Noke's eyes widened as she noticed it. It was of a man with a sword held aloft in a deathly still pose. Noke had seen the picture before and felt the same eerie sensation. *Where do I know him from?* She squinted, trying to puzzle it out and then, like a sound from the silence – it hit her all at once. She knew who she was looking at.

Noke doubled over, dropping to one knee. Her breathing came in short sharp gasps and she found her heart was thumping against her chest with painful force.

"What is it?" Kasa asked, frowning at her.

Noke glanced up at the picture and her voice came out breathy and low. "Father."

CHAPTER FIVE

The man who sat at the center of the trio – the boyish one; cleared his throat and silence fell. When he spoke, his voice tolled like a bell in Noke's chest. She shuddered at the sound of it. *What a voice.*

"I call the conclave to order," he said.

It was as though his voice came from somewhere deep in the earth. The sort of voice you would hear at a village play, where someone plays the part of Ebisu, god of fortune. Full, thick and ominous. Like the sound of a hammer on an anvil.

Finally, he raised his chin to meet Noke's gaze.

"Introduce yourself."

Noke felt her mouth dry up and all the bubbling words she had seemed to wither to mist on her tongue. "I...I...," she gathered herself and bunched up a fist. "I am Nokemono."

"And why have you come here?" the man asked.

Nokemono drew in a breath. "I am here to become a warrior. To wield the sword Kazeshini."

A smile quirked at the corner of the boyish one's lips and he looked to the grandfatherly one. "I told you this would be interesting."

The older man frowned and gave Noke an appraising look. "Who is your father?"

Noke's jaw tightened. "I have no father."

The older man narrowed his eyes. "Only the gods have no father. Are you a god child?"

"No," Noke said, biting down on her lip. "I meant that I do not know who my father is."

The boyish one pointed towards the painting behind her. "Do you know who that is?"

Noke looked up at the picture, taking in each detail of the face in it. She knew who it was, who it had to be, and yet she knew that was not the right answer to give.

She shook her head. "No."

The boyish man nodded. "That is Yamato Cen. He was a great warrior. One of the greatest."

Noke felt her heart fall at the word 'was'. "Is he dead?" she asked.

The boyish man narrowed his eyes. "We do not know for sure."

"I see," Noke said.

He leaned forward and gave Noke a hard, inspecting look. "Do you recognize the man in that picture at all?"

Noke squinted. "A little, I guess."

The boyish man gave the others a satisfied nod. "My name is Ikeda Cen. I am an acolyte to the Master Spiritual."

Noke bowed low. If this man was an acolyte to the Master Spiritual, then it meant he was one of the highest-ranking monks in the temple. Even for one as stubborn as

Noke, there is a time to show reverence and give honor to those to whom it is due. She pressed her palms to the floor in the most formal prostate salute and bowed her head. "It is good to meet you."

He gave a half-smile. "Tell me, why should we admit you into our temple? From what I hear, you have tried twice to steal from this place and yet to bow before us, asking that we teach you. Why should we accept you?"

Noke lowered her chin and pondered her answer for a long moment. The conclave observed a watchful silence, each waiting for what she had to say.

The older man cleared his throat. "We do not have all day, girl," he hissed. "Give us one good reason. Of why we shouldn't throw you out of this place."

Noke narrowed her eyes and took in a breath. "I am many things, Masters. I have been a thief of the rich and visitors, a destroyer of hopes and dreams, a relentless savage that has beaten people till they couldn't stand." She hesitated. "I have cheated people. I have fallen short in the sight of the gods," she paused, gathering herself, "and despite all that I have done, the gods brought me here, to a room with you. Even when I am brought low, I am reminded on days like this," she hesitated, "that I can be brought high."

Ikeda nodded approvingly.

I might not be perfect, but I'm still here! Noke said "I came here to make something. I climbed a mountain. I engaged in combat with men two times my senior. With hope in my heart, I took the hard path, knowing that someone would be there to make it easier. With powerful hands, willing ears, and honest endeavor, I built a new life by braving the perils of a wild world. I am tired of doing wrong," she dropped to one knee, "accept me, Masters, so I can start to do right."

The conclave was utterly silent for a long moment. The only sound in the room was the sharp intake of Noke's breathing as she gathered herself.

Ikeda was the first to speak. "You have heard it for yourselves. The girl speaks wisdom."

The bearded monk nodded. "She does."

The old man shook his head. "There is a difference between cunning and wisdom. I had no doubts that the girl is cunning, but I will not be too quick to call it wisdom. She is yet to convince me."

Ikeda nodded. "And I. There is still more before I am so convinced."

The bearded monk nodded his agreement. "I as well."

Ikeda turned back to Noke. "Tanto tells me that you have tattoos on your back."

Noke gave a deferent bow. "Yes, I do."

"Show them to us."

She turned her back to them, hiking up the hem of her kimono until they could see her markings clearly.

Ikeda Cen gasped and the grandfatherly one rose to his feet, muttering a prayer.

Nokemono glanced over her shoulder at them, slowly letting her shirt fall back into place. They looked for the first time, afraid.

"What is it?" she asked.

Ikeda Cen gave her a pitying look. "Now is not the time to ask questions, child. For now, you are only to give us answers."

The grandfatherly monk stirred in his seat and made a disgusted noise in his throat. "Some may be too young to remember, but I am not. We have had impostors before. Many of them. Hoping to find a shortcut in our sacred way. I am not convinced by this charlatan girl."

Ikeda Cen raised his chin. "Do you not see the tattoos on her back?"

The older man waved it away. "Easily done. There are many who know how to imitate our markings. A skilled counterfeiter can produce the same spotless work within an hour of payment."

Ikeda Cen shook his head and looked at the third man, the big one. "What say you Kato?"

Kato leaned back in his seat and fixed Noke with his dark eyes. "It is true what Hara says. She may be a charlatan, but it is also possible that she is not. We have no way of knowing."

Ikeda Cen snorted. "So, we should do nothing, like we always do."

Kato shook his head. "I did not say we should do nothing."

"What are you saying, then?"

"We should test her. Let us know if she has the character to be one of us."

"She is a woman," the older man Hara snapped.

"And we have trained women before. She would not be the first to be admitted here."

"And each one has been a mistake. They are not built to withstand the training to be one of us. They are not resilient enough."

Noke scowled. "Try me, old man," she spat.

All three men glanced at her in shock. She had barely realized what she was saying before she had spoken.

"She reveals herself," Hara snarled. "Insolent, full of pride, ill disciplined."

"As we all have been at some time in our lives, one need not be a saint to be accepted in this house. If that were the case, not one of us would be here," Ikeda said, "or have we forgotten that?"

A moment of silence fell.

Kato pointed to Kasa. "What say you Kasa? You have spent time with the girl, at least. What is your opinion?"

Kasa straightened, plainly surprised to have been called upon by the council. He drew himself up to his full height and raised his chin.

"I stand with you, Master Kato. Let us put her to the test."

Kato arched an eyebrow. "What sort of test would you propose? She knows nothing of our teachings and cannot be expected to engage in a test of combat against any of our other students. Even if we could find one of her size and age, it would be a horrible mismatch."

Kasa nodded. "Even in a mismatched fight, the truth of a person can be revealed. Adversity is a great destroyer of masks. Put her in a fight she cannot win and we will know who she truly is."

Ikeda narrowed his head in disappointment, but Kato raised his chin in approval. "You speak wisely, Kasa."

Ikeda lowered his head. His face was grave. "Though I hate to say it – it is true. You speak wisely, Kasa."

Kato gave a deep nod. "A test of combat may not be enough. What of her intellect? Her focus. Her resilience."

Ikeda nodded. "Three tests. One of intelligence. One of character and the last of valor in combat."

Hara quirked his lip in half-satisfaction. "I agree."

Ikeda raised his fist. "So, it is settled, then. We will test her in three ways. Intelligence. Character and valor in combat."

A few moments later, Tanto stepped back into the room. The student he had brought was a scrawny, long-limbed boy who looked at least a year younger than Noke. He looked as if he hadn't eaten in days and walked with the hunched-back, ground-glaring slouch of a person accustomed to disappointment. Noke thought she could take him, but with the warning Ikeda had given her, her heart still thumped in her chest. She tried to meet the boy's eye, but he was oblivious to her.

Hara stepped into the room and gave an approving look. Plainly he had been involved in picking this particular boy – a boy who barely looked like he could subdue a cat and had no physical advantage over Noke. The man wanted a humiliation of such proportion that Noke would have no future chance to return to the temple.

Ikeda turned to Kasa. "You shall be the umpire. The first test shall be her test of intelligence."

CHAPTER SIX

Tanto brought in a small table with two equally small wooden stools. Noke tried to make eye contact with the boy, but he pointedly avoided her. She had the feeling that he was irritated to be matched up against a girl. It must have been some kind of insult to be judged the closest to her level.

For one moment, their eyes met and Noke offered a hand.

He stared at her hand as if it was thick with leprosy, gave a disgusted snort and turned back to the table Tanto had set up.

"Sit," Kasa commanded.

Noke's opponent moved first to take the further of the two stools. Noke slid into the vacant one.

A large, wooden board had been set down in between them board composed of rectangles in a grid of nine ranks. Noke stifled a quiet smile. *Shogi.*

Noke had learned how to play Shogi from the wiliest sort alive – market woman. More than once, Noke had won some money off an old trader or arrogant merchant who thought they could make an example out of her. She knew the fabric of the game. Knew how to anticipate opponent's moves and capitalize on them. If this was to be her test, then she knew she would make quick work of the boy in front of her.

Her opponent was almost casually confident. He stared at the board with no greater scrutiny than one would his own hand. Plainly, he had some skill at the game too and was just as certain as she.

"You know the game?" Kasa asked, setting down the pieces.

Noke nodded. "Yes."

Kasa narrowed his eyes. "Good." He stepped down from the table and folded his arms. "You may begin."

Noke glanced down at the board, almost licking her lips with delight. She noticed the pieces on her side and gave a start.

"There are pieces missing. My side is not complete."

Kasa nodded. "You are over-matched. This is a test of intelligence, not of your ability to play Shogi. You must show how you use your intelligence to overcome an obstacle."

Noke scowled as she stared down at the board. "That is not fair."

Kasa wet his lips. "If you came here looking for fairness, perhaps you are a charlatan after all."

Noke felt her toes curl up in her sandals as she stared down at the board. It was a hopeless situation. She had only one gold general, no silver generals and just one knight instead of two. The boy, on the other hand had his full complement of pieces.

The masters of the conclave watched the game with eager attention, each one of them eyeing the board with unwavering focus.

Noke tried to think for a moment, then threw up her hands. "How on earth am I supposed to win?"

Kasa pointed to his head. "I don't know. You are the one who is being tested."

Noke's left hand curled up into a fist as she studied the board and tried to reason her best move. "Fine," she hissed.

She moved a pawn forward.

The boy opposite her arched an eyebrow, then mirrored her move.

Noke jabbed a golden general into the opening space. With an almost irritating calm, the boy moved his lance forward and snatched up her piece.

Noke seethed. The boy was sharp. It was a reckless move, but only a skilled player would have the wit and wherewithal to punish her so quickly. She slumped back in her stool, half wanting to flip the board over.

She glanced over her shoulder and saw Hara's keen anticipatory look. He could see her failing and was loving it.

Kasa stood deathly still. If he had any opinion on the matter, he didn't show it.

Noke reached for another pawn, then stopped herself short. *Think. Think.*

She was outnumbered, over-matched and short of options. She reached out for her knight and stopped herself. The boy, seated opposite, watched her keenly, awaiting her next move with the effortless grace of a grandfather. It was a matter of time before her game was done.

Hara cleared his throat and whispered loud enough for everyone in the room to hear. "What does a rat do when it is caught in a trap?"

"I am not a rat," Noke spat.

"What did you say?" Hara asked.

"I said I am not a rat!"

She pushed a knight forward in a deft maneuver. The boy countered it immediately with his lance. Noke moved aggressively, supporting the knight with a pawn. The boy defended his piece with a pawn of his own.

Noke smiled. "Just as I thought, they brought me the only warrior monk with no courage."

The boy's eyes teetered with a flash of emotion. Her words had hit the mark.

He responded to her with an attack on her left flank. Noke frowned as she saw he had her pressed on both sides.

The boy allowed himself a smile but said nothing.

She sat back on her stool, staring down at the board as though it was a book with words impossible to understand. With her jaw tightening, she pushed her knight forward again. It was a dangerously aggressive move that left her open to a vicious counterattack.

Almost as soon as she dropped her piece, the boy went on the offensive. He brought his silver general into the fight and moved into the space. The boy took a pawn first, then another on his next move and, at the last, a lance. He had seen her weakness and exploited it immediately.

Hara leaned forward, studying the game, then his lips curled into a triumphant smile. He straightened in his chair and spoke in that poorly disguised whisper.

"To be a warrior in this temple, you must have the wit to think ahead. Far, far ahead. Even when the odds are against you, you must never resort to cheap, empty aggression. That is the way of street rats."

Noke felt the vein throb at her neck as she launched a weak effort at defending what was already defeated on her left side. Another reckless move.

Noke swore aloud.

"She reveals herself," Hara said. "Foul language."

His voice was thick with smugness. He enjoyed watching her unravel.

The boy, buoyed by Hara's boasts of encouragement, decimated her left side. He didn't just want to end the game; he wanted to humiliate Noke.

Noke brought her lance forward, and the boy ate it up. He looked at her with a look verging on pity. "Do you give up?"

Hara muttered his approval. "Yes, perhaps we should end the farce."

Noke stared down at the board with a look of utter defeat, then lifted her chin to meet her opponent's eyes. As she looked up, her lips curled into a smile. She reached for a piece without even needing to look down.

"You spoke wisdom, Master Hara," Noke began, picking up a pawn. "To be a warrior in this temple, you must have the wit to think ahead. Far, far ahead."

She took out her opponent's silver general.

The boy frowned.

Noke's smile widened. "Even when the odds are against you, you must never resort to cheap, empty aggression."

She took out his knight with another pawn.

The boy stared down at the board, his eyes narrow with outrage and tried to defend his king, but it was too late. He had fallen into her trap.

"What did you call it, Master Hara?" Noke said, sliding her final pawn into place. "The way of street rats."

With that, she rammed the victory home, flicking the king piece from the board with a casual snap of her finger.

No painter, no sculptor, no skilled weaver of cloth could produce a picture quite as furious as Hara's face. His dull pale skin had surged with color as he realized that Noke had won. She hadn't needed to humiliate him, but calling her a street rat was the move that had made her mind up.

She rose from the table and smiled amidst the stupefied silence. "You truly spoke wisdom, Master Kasa. You said even in a mismatched fight, the truth of a person can be revealed. Adversity is a great destroyer of masks. There you have it, Master Hara. There is no mask now. See me for what I am. I am no rat. I am a lion."

She kicked the stool down and stretched cat-like at the center of the room. "So I suppose that is my intelligence test done. What next?"

Ikeda looked impressed. Kato looked intrigued but Hara looked horrified.

"I think we have seen enough of her character," Kato offered.

Hara narrowed his eyes. "Let's go straight to the fight, then."

Kasa nodded and moved to the center of the room. With a small stick of chalk, he drew an uneven circle around the room. Then he gestured for Noke and the other student to step close.

"You will fight in this circle," Kasa said, "keep it simple. Obey my instructions at all times."

The other student gave a lazy nod and yawned as he looked Noke up and down. Something about the casual indifference of his yawn sent a sliver of irritation up Noke's spine. Though she had no real formal training, she was sure she'd seen more fights in half her life than the dopey boy had in twice his own. When it came to taking a beating, she had years of experience and from men far more dangerous than him. She gritted her teeth. *I am not going to surrender. No matter what.*

"Are you listening to me?" Kasa asked.

Only then did Noke realize he had been talking. She waved dismissively. "Yes."

Kasa gave her an infuriated look, then rolled his eyes. "Very well." He stepped out from the circle. "You go when I say you do."

The boy nodded slowly, and his eyes narrowed with serious concentration. It only took a moment, but the transformation was palpable. The boy straightened and tilted his neck till it made a clicking sound, then stretched forward to touch his toes. His eyes, which had seemed vacant and uninterested, were suddenly calm and calculated. As he stretched, Noke noticed that his arms, though skinny, were kneaded with lumps of muscle. His chin had the chiseled sharpness of a man twice his age and he moved with legs always spread apart, his balance almost perfect. Make no mistake, he was a fighter. To make matters worse – she had humiliated him.

She glanced over at Hara. He mouthed a single word noiselessly, "Die."

"Now!" Ikeda shouted.

The fight began.

<u>CHAPTER SEVEN</u>

Her opponent sprung to life. His speed was so sudden and unanticipated that Noke stumbled, trying to jump back. It was a lucky thing, for his first blow only grazed the underside of her chin as she fell.

With a perfect reaction, the boy sprang forward again. It wasn't just that he was fast; it was that he was precise. He knew exactly where he needed to be in a fight and got there with an almost spiritual instinct. If this was a dance, he had heard the music before, knew all the moves, and she was barely trying to stay on tempo. If it were a song, he knew the words, played the music and had written a verse of his own. By contrast, she could barely catch the tune. As Noke tried to step back from him, he folded his leg around hers and gave her a small push.

She fell back. Her head smacked hard against the ground and the breath rushed out of her. The boy looked down at her through half-lidded eyes and arched an eyebrow as though to ask a question. 'Is that enough?', his eyes seemed to say. Noke tried to get up but a flush of pain stabbed through her back. She shut her eyes and tried to breathe.

The boy began walking away. He thought the fight was done.

Now was a good time to surrender. She had taken a blow to the head, but nothing she would struggle to recover from. There was no shame in surrender to the superior fighter.

She glanced up at the table where the members of the conclave sat. They were all unimpressed, but not surprised. She was about to turn away when she saw the eager, justified smile of the old man Hara. The sheer smugness of the man-made Noke scowl.

"Do you surrender?" Kasa asked, staring down at her.

Noke's response came in a low growl. "No."

The boy stopped in his tracks at the sound of her voice and glanced back over his shoulder.

Noke needed no invitation to use her suddenness. She launched herself to her feet and went after the boy, who now stood at the edge of the circle.

He gave her a surprised look as she shot towards him. With a slick sidestep, he dodged out of the way as she flung herself at him. Without waiting, she punched left, then right, tiring quickly as she went after him. The boy avoided the flurry with the consummate ease of a father brushing his baby aside. Ikeda was right – she had little chance.

But a little chance was all she needed. The boy was stronger, faster, better trained, more disciplined and surrounded by friends. It *was* a mismatch.

But Noke was a street girl. She'd seen more barroom brawls than square meals and had faced down worse odds in every day of her life. She went at the boy again, this time abandoning every illusion of honor.

As she went to kick his leg, he arched it back to dodge. Noke turned her kick into a knee and stepped forward to knee him in the crotch. He doubled over and gave a low wheeze for air, catching his breath.

She saw his face changed as he winced. He was used to fighting his fellow students. Disciplined warrior monks to be. He knew nothing of a dirty, ugly fight – a fight in which there is no honor and there are no prizes. As well trained as he was, he had no experience fighting with someone who saw honor as a long-dead lie. He had never been in the sort of knuckle down scrap that made a reputation out of local taprooms.

Smiling, she punched his armpit and curled her fingers to pull his armpit hairs as she drew her hand back. He grunted, showing his disapproval but did not let up with his perfect attacks. Noke fought like a cornered scavenger animal. Nothing was too sneaky for her. She pulled his hair, stubbed his toe, bit his elbow, aimed for his most sensitive places. The only thing which matched his surprise was his outrage – he simply couldn't believe a young woman could fight as Noke did and get away with it. With each low blow, he got enraged and soon his warrior's cool gave way to schoolboy petulance. He didn't just want to beat Noke; he wanted to hurt her. That she could use.

From there, every action she took was with the intent to provoke, embarrass and humiliate her opponent. She mimicked him by dragging her knuckles along the ground and making sounds to mock him. She hated having to treat the boy that way, but this was the only chance she had.

He started swinging wildly, missing wide and barely making Noke work. The fight was turning now, and the man was tiring quickly.

"Is this the best you can offer here?" Noke taunted, "a dopey brat?"

The boy's only facial reaction to the jibe was a slight narrowing of the eyes. His attacks, however, seemed to get more predictable after that. He was going for the jugular and was leaving multiple openings, as he did for Noke to exploit. She tested a few casual attacks and had some success. It wasn't until she had tagged him half a dozen times realizing how much of a chance she had.

Just as Noke began believing she had the measure of her opponent, she got overconfident and danced too close to the fire. The big brute he caught her about the wrist as she tried to slip a punch and pulled her close into an embrace. "No more games," he hissed quietly to her.

He grabbed her neck with both hands and lifted her off the ground. He had twenty times her strength. As he slowly started pressing down on her throat stone, Noke scratched at his wrist. She gritted her teeth and tried to fight back, but it was no use. He had her.

"I surrender," she whispered.

The boy didn't stop. He kept pressing.

Noke's eyes bulged. "I surrender," she hissed, but her words came out in a dribbling, choking mess. No one but him would hear her, and he had suddenly gone deaf. She looked into his eyes and saw murder in them.

She tried to suck in a breath, but the pressure was incredible. Her eyes went blurry with tears as her hands fell limp at her side. The last thing she saw was the resolution in his eyes – then she passed out.

She heard voices mutter as the world went black but couldn't pick out a single word they were saying. In a moment of pure instinct, she reached for the side of his head and struck out with a pang of force. Somehow, in some act of forgotten skill – it hit the mark and his grip on her throat slackened. Bubbles of colored light blurred her vision as she tried to suck in air.

She coughed up blood and steadied herself. "You'll have to do better than that."

Her opponent moved with clumsy speed, and Noke saw that he was staggered by her strike. She moved to corner him, stepping in a wide circle to close the range while maintaining a safe distance.

Left with nothing but the rage to hold onto, the boy charged at her. This time there was nothing held back. Noke was ready for him. She let her weight slink onto her trailing foot, poised for a counterstrike. They fell in a rolling tangle and somehow her opponent landed on top.

The boy brought his fist down with accumulated malice. The first blow was so hard, Noke thought he would crack his skull open. Blood gushed from the open wound above her eye. *I am going to die.*

Through the bloodied vision, she saw Tanto drag the boy off her.

She tried to stand, but collapsed again in a bloodied heap. She had done her best, given him all he was asking for. Though she had been defeated, she had shown herself. She wasn't easy meat and all the conclave would know – that was enough. She coughed out another spurt of blood, then rolled onto her back as her eyes closed.

Noke woke to the sound of crickets bleating. She sat up. The moon loomed above in a naked, starless sky. She glanced over her shoulder. Only then did she notice Tanto, who sat cross-legged on the floor. Beside him was a large round swathe of ragged cloth.

She turned towards him, eyes alight with eagerness. "Did I make it? Did the conclave accept me?"

Tanto frowned. "I suppose, in a manner of speaking, they did."

"What do you mean?" Noke asked.

"You were defeated. Set you one last test. Beat this one and you have no further troubles with the matter."

"What is the test?"

The whisper of a smile curled on Tanto's lips. "They call it the Breaking."

"Why?" Noke asked.

"I suppose you will see about that," he said with a laugh that was almost villainous. "

"What do I have to do?" Noke asked instead.

"Simple," Tanto began, "you climb to the summit of the mountain and then come back down."

"It sounds fairly easy."

"It does, doesn't it?" Tanto said, smiling. "It really does."

Something about Tanto's ebullient smile let Noke know this new task was far from easy. "There is something you aren't telling me, isn't there?"

He smiled and unraveled the cloth beside him. A large metal disk shone in the light, twined with a thick hemp rope. "You'll be carrying this all the way."

Noke's head fell. *There's always a catch with you damned monks.*

CHAPTER EIGHT

Pain is an irritating travel companion. From head to toe, Noke felt pain. Her whole body was like one contiguous bruise. She let none of it show. She wouldn't give Tanto the opportunity to report her as weak.

"How are you feeling?" Tanto asked, smiling.

It was a smile that brought no warmth. The smile of a crocodile or a tiger. A wicked, predatory smile.

Noke suppressed a scowl as she glanced down at the large metal disk that hung from the rope around her neck. "Never felt better," she hissed through strained breaths.

They had been climbing for less than an hour and the trek was already almost unbearable. Tanto had a large stick in his hand that he swept across the grass as they walked.

He stepped out in front of her, setting a murderous pace. "Patience, diligence, resilience and concentration. All these things are what you must learn if you wish to become one of us."

"You forgot to add craziness," Noke muttered.

Tanto's stick lashed out at her and she dodged with a drop of the head.

He smiled. "You learn fast."

Noke's jaw tightened. "What is the point of all this? I have completed your tasks. What more do you want from me? This is cruel."

"I thought you said you wish to wield the Wind of Death?"

She lowered her eyes. "I do."

"Then this is necessary, Nokemono. If you truly wish to be admitted into our order and learn to wield a weapon of such great power, then you must understand the responsibility that comes with it."

Noke frowned as they continued to climb and muttered under her breath. "Whatever."

Tanto stopped and glanced over his shoulder at her. "If you wish to stop, all you have to do is say the word and we can return to the village."

Noke considered that for a moment. The sweet relief of removing the weight from her neck for a time felt like a temptation worth throwing every other dream away. But she had come too far, lost too much already. This was it. "I will never quit."

Tanto arched an eyebrow. "Then act like it. I won't have you sulking like an infant every time I tell you to do something you think is unpleasant."

Noke's eyes widened. "Alright."

She gritted her teeth, bunched up her fists and kept walking. Tanto went ahead and, before long, she could barely see him as they ascended the mountain. After an hour, she fell into something of a trance – counting each step as a triumph. She didn't look up at the mountain. The only thing she concentrated on was the next step. So long as she could take one step, she could continue.

Her breath came in short sharp gasps and she felt as though her neck would break under the weight of the disk, but she kept going. *Just one step at a time.*

She had lost all sense of time and place when a voice called out to her ahead.

"Who are you?"

Noke raised her chin and glanced up. A man stood ahead. He had a beard which extended all the way to his stomach and wore a homespun white kimono dotted with blotches of red.

Tanto was nowhere to be seen.

With an effort, Noke straightened and met the man's gaze. "My name is Nokemono."

The man's eyes softened as he gave her a longer, appraising look. He stepped forward a few paces, staring all the while at the metal disk that was strapped around her neck.

"You have reached the summit," he said with a knowing look.

Noke looked around. He was right. The ground was level here and there was nothing above them but the clouds.

He stepped close and touched the metal disk, running his palm over it as though trying to feel for some secret message. His eyes widened as he looked down at her.

"Welcome warrior," he said, "your trial is almost over."

Noke narrowed her eyes. "Almost?"

He gave her the same crocodile smile that she had seen Tanto give.

She cleared her throat. "Where is Tanto?"

"Patience child. He will join you soon." He cleared his throat and straightened. "Come with me. We have much to discuss."

Noke stared for a moment before deciding to follow the strange man. He didn't look dangerous.

She followed him into a small cave carved into the face of giant rock where a pot of soup boiled over above a cookfire.

The man opened his clenched fist above the cooking pot to reveal crushed flowers. He sprinkled the flowers into the soup and stirred with a long wooden spoon.

"Have some," he said, holding the pot out to her "…for the pain".

Noke nuzzled the bowl back with an upturned hand.

"Don't worry, it won't hurt you," he said, taking a short sip for himself.

Noke stared down into the pot. The liquid was a bright purple with a thin cloud of vapor rising above it. Under any other circumstances, she would have refused but there was something strangely alluring about the aroma that made her act against her natural instincts. She took the bowl and drank deep.

"What is your name?" she asked. "I told you mine."

The man's smile spread wide across his face. "I have been called many, many names, but you can call me Aana."

Noke stared down at the now empty bowl. "What did you give me?" suddenly feeling stupid for drinking it.

"Don't you feel it?" he asked.

She frowned as her stomach groaned. "No."

Aana wet his lips. "Just give it a moment."

Nothing happened at first. Nothing besides Aana's smile. Then Noke could feel herself breathing. Not in the way she normally did. This was as though he was astride a great bird, watching herself breathe from a distance. Breathing was beautiful.

She heard Aana laughing somewhere, but he was far away from her and his laughter could not penetrate the wall of bliss around her. The gentle breeze on her skin made it tingle with joy. She reveled in the ground beneath her sandals, the taste of the air, the soft brush of wind through the cavern opening. She looked to the cookfire and saw faces gone forever. Akari, Hinadori, her mother, her father. When she saw them, they did not bring her pain, instead they brought her relief, clarity.

Akari glanced up at her and smiled. "Keep going," Akari said. "You are doing well."

Hinadori looked away; his cheeks flushing with shame as he looked away.

Her mother and father stood as one, with hands locked. Her father towered over her mother and had the unmistakable bearing of a warrior. Shoulders back, chin raised, sword balancing as easily on his hip as a dinner plate on the table. Her mother, though shorter, matched his aura. She was every inch the noble queen, her eyes softening as she set her eyes on Noke and smiling a word of encouragement.

"Keep going," her father said.

His words were like warm bread in her mouth. They nourished her in ways she could not imagine. Nokemono blinked once more and all the faces were gone.

She was still hot inside and calm like a stone beneath running water. Noke was light on her feet, nimble as a cat.

"How do you feel?" Aana asked.

Noke fumbled for the right words and found herself on the brink of laughing out loud. "Still... and clear. Whole. What did you give me?"

"It is called the Jidakippo poppy. It will help you connect to your higher self."

"How long will I feel like this?"

"Long enough for me to teach you a thing or two about the path you have chosen to tread."

Aana took her by the hand. "Follow my instruction."

Using his hands, he bent her down to parabola until she felt an aching stretch at the back of her calf.

"Hold this pose," he instructed.

Noke gritted her teeth. "Easier said than done."

Aana's laughter came from deep in his throat. "To become an instrument of the higher ones, you must be like water. Fluid. Yield to your pain, become soft like water so that when the hard knife strikes you gain no wound, it is in a softness that the water triumphs over the hardness of the knife."

"What do you mean?"

"All the world is energy and you must allow yourself to channel it by learning to commit all your focus to a single center-point. Jidakippo will help you find the center."

"I –,"

"Shhh," urged Aana, pulling her hands forward until her back started shaking. "Like water."

Noke did her best to follow the choreography and found herself lost to the euphoria of the Jidakippo. It had an overwhelming effect that made everything seem possible. All her pain was gone, all her worry was gone, all her hate was gone. The only thing left was joy. Pure as the living water.

Seconds seemed to stretch into hours until all concept of time slipped from her hands like sand. She could feel herself beginning to find an overwhelming sense of focus.

"Good," said Aana. "Now tell me, what do you want?"

It seemed clear to Noke. "I want to wield Kazeshini. The Wind of Death."

Aana shook his head. "What do you want more deeply than that?"

Noke furrowed her brow. "To prove everyone wrong."

Aana hissed in irritation. "Deeper."

"To prove myself. To know that I am more than just a street rat."

"Deeper!"

Noke saw it plain, the truth of her condition. The truth that she had been running from for so much of her life. Which drove her every action and reaction. She gathered in a breath.

"Say it," Aana shouted.

Noke's confession came in a low whisper. "To make my father proud."

The words left her with a gust of strength and she fell limp to the side as soon as the words were said. She felt energy from the ground start to ripple through her body, building as the earth seemed to rumble.

"Good," Aana said, pulling up her chin and arching her back towards the top of the cave.

"Can you feel it?" Aana asked.

"Yes," Noke confirmed.

"Now say these words after me. 'Watashi no senzo no kami. Watashitachi no tsumi o yurushi kudasai.'"

Noke gritted her teeth and spoke aloud. "Watashi no senzo no kami. Watashitachi no tsumi o yurushi kudasai."

A blinding flash of white rendered all eyesight nugatory as a torrent of energy built within Noke. It lasted only a moment, then it was gone. Quick as a kiss.

Aana began to clap. "Well done. Come with me."

He led her deeper into the cave, where he had a well of black ink and a long silver needle. He produced a dark burlap sack with a thick case inside. The sort of case which might have kept a game of mahjong.

Noke narrowed her eyes. The case was no game or plaything.

Aana unlocked the latches on each end of the case, and it flipped open in a beautiful flourish. As the lid was pulled back, the many trays inside lifted and fanned out, displaying the full gamut of his instruments. There were at least a dozen blades of every size and shape, needles curved and straight. Next to them were vials of clear liquid marked with inked inscription, hammers, chisels. Metal, wood and glass glittered in the light, all polished to a murderous sheen and oiled in anticipation of good use.

Noke frowned. "What are you doing?"

Aana ignored her question. "Give me your hand."

Noke edged away from him. "Why?"

He sighed. "I have to mark your hand," he said, picking out a needle and dipping it into the ink bottle. "So, the conclave will know you have seen me."

Noke reluctantly extended her hand. Aana seized her by the wrist and made a small inscription on her forearm with the point of the needle. The pain was sharp but instantly ebbed away as he made his mark.

"There," he said, admiring his work. "Now you can return to the temple."

"I have to climb all the way down?"

Aana shook his head, the whisper of a smile at the corner of his lips. "There's a shortcut."

He led Noke out through the cave mouth and down a winding footpath which led to the edge of the mountain.

"Your time here is done and now we complete your breaking," Aana said.

Noke arched an eyebrow. "Where is Tanto? You said he would join me."

Aana smiled his crocodile smile once again. "He will join you at the bottom."

Noke gave him a confused look. "What do you mean by…?"

Without warning, Aana gave her a hard shove, and she toppled over the edge of the cliff. The fear hit her so hard that her heart almost burst as she the wind rushed past her. She screamed, but could barely hear herself over the urgent knock of blood thumping in her ears. Her eyes widened as she realized she was falling. Falling from a height no one should fall from. Falling to her death.

The scream died in her throat and she closed her eyes. Her torn kimono billowing and slapping against her skin as the world somersaulted around her. Hot wind roared in her face as she tumbled through the air.

A thought came to her that had come many times. This time, it felt painfully true. She dragged in a breath and steadied herself, her body still becalmed by the Jidakippo and said her last prayer. *I am going to die.*

CHAPTER NINE

Pain is a teacher. As the ground raced towards her, Noke anticipated a new and unparalleled lesson. She clattered into a tree, hitting each branch as she went down. Twigs scratched and tore at her as she plunged down. Then she hit a grass strewn net which gave way, breaking her fall as she tumbled forward. When she hit the ground, she felt no pain. Her entire body went instantly numb and for a moment, the only thing she saw was a tree-shaped cloud in the sky. Then a figure appeared at the corner of her vision.

Tanto smiled down at her. "Sometimes you have to break the hard shell to get to the true fruit."

Then the pain came. Her left hand was twisted at a horrible angle, purpled and swollen. Her right leg looked like she had taken a bath in blood. She tried to move her neck, but the pain slapped her down. The pain hit her so thumping hard that it nearly made her vomit. She wanted to curse at Tanto but couldn't move her tongue to form the words.

"Don't try to move," Tanto said. "It isn't time for that yet". He produced a small glass vial and held it up to the light.

Blood dribbled from Noke's mouth as Tanto curled his hand around her teeth and pulled her jaw open. He opened the vial and poured the contents down her throat.

Noke recognized the taste instantly. It was Jiddakippo. Her tongue seemed to tighten and then relax at the taste as that euphoric relief passed up through her veins.

"If you are to wield the Wind of Death. You must know to respect the wind. When a tree tries to fight the wind and refuses to bend, it is broken for its trouble."

Noke gritted her teeth, garbling blood as she forced four words out. "I will kill you."

Tanto smiled. "Not today."

With that, he carefully pulled her into his arms and started the walk back to the temple, cradling her as one would a baby.

Noke's heart pounded with the urgent thump of a girl at door's death. She didn't know who to blame, who to hate. All she knew was that she wanted the pain to stop.

Tanto took her to a small room in the temple and lay her down on a thick bed mat. "I know how you must feel. You hate us right now, but this is all for the best. You will come back stronger and more whole than you ever were before you were broken."

Noke could only manage to stare up at the man, hoping her eyes would convey the inward promise she was making to kill him.

One monk placed a white cloth over her eyes. The hissing sound of billowing smoke whispered against her ear and she caught a hint of burning incense at the tip of her tongue. The drowsiness came almost immediately after. Sleep calling her name loud as a parent.

"You will come back stronger," came Tanto's voice as she felt herself slipping away.

I had better.

*

When Noke woke, her mouth was desperately dry. She wet her lips, and they tasted like chalk. All the pain was gone. It was like she had arisen from a year-long slumber and only now sucking in clean air. As her eyes snapped open, she immediately glanced down at her hand. The last time she had looked at it, her knuckles were broken and her fist was mangled and purple. Now it looked like the hand of a stranger; and not just any stranger – she had the soft, firm hands of potter.

The sight of her hand made her gasp and she jerked upright in her bed mat. She was alone in the room but could still feel the lingering presence of recent human activity. Someone had been there a short time long ago.

Just then, the door slid open and a short, balding monk stepped inside with a bowl and white cloth.

He gave a start when he saw Noke sitting upright. "You're awake."

Noke tilted her neck until it clicked and smacked her lips together. "Where is Tanto?"

The monk gave her a nervous look and opened his mouth to answer.

A tall figure stepped into the room, filling the doorway as he slid inside.

"I am here," Tanto said, his eyes fixed on Noke.

The monk looked from Tanto to Noke with a face of worry. "We had not expected her to awaken for at least another day."

Tanto smiled. "I figured she would surprise us. This one is born of old blood. The sort that never sits still."

"She may not be ready," the monk cautioned.

Tanto stepped closer. "Nonsense. How do you feel, Nokemono?"

Noke stretched cat-like on her bed mat, arching her toes and rolling her shoulders. "I feel amazing," she said honestly.

Tanto nodded to the monk. "She is ready. I know she is."

The monk set his bowl down and gave Tanto a reproachful glare. "She will have another day of rest. Let her body fully heal. I will go straight to the Master Spiritual if you try to take her from here."

Tanto frowned. "Fine. Tomorrow then."

The monk gave a nod of petulant triumph and brought the bowl to Noke's lips. "Drink."

Noke arched an eyebrow. "What is it?"

The monk rolled his eyes. "I liked you better when you were still unconscious. Drink," he insisted.

Noke sniffed at the bowl, drew in a breath and then took a sip. There was Jiddakippo in it, but there were other herbs too that gave it a tougher edge. She drained the rest of the content and felt her body slip into an easy relaxation.

"Good," the monk said. He glanced up at Tanto, then moved towards the door. "I'll give you a moment."

Tanto nodded as the other monk slipped out of the room. He stepped close to Noke and let out a calm breath. "I am sure you are wondering why you were pushed off the edge of a mountain."

Noke lowered her chin. "That's one thing I am wondering, yes."

"We had to do it," Tanto said. "I too once fell from that same height. It is essential that the most stubborn amongst us endure the Breaking."

"What if I had died?"

Tanto narrowed his eyes. "We rarely lose people."

"But you have lost people before dropping them?" Noke asked.

Tanto lowered his head. "Yes, we have."

For a long moment, Noke was silent. Then she firmed her lips and spoke in a low whisper. "That is unforgivable."

Tanto straightened. "It is not for you to tell what the gods will and will not forgive Noke. The Breaking is an important part of our tradition. When our flesh and bone are broken, it teaches us that our bodies are fallible, fragile and impermanent. The spiritual triumphs over the temporal, always. That is something you will always need to remember in your time here at the temple."

Noke glanced at her once disfigured hand. "Couldn't you find some simpler, less lethal way of making that simple point?"

"It is not for me to question the wisdom of age-old tradition."

Noke narrowed her eyes. "Is that what you all are here, then? Mumblers who never question the humanity of your traditions? Are you not allowed to have an opinion as a monk?"

"Every monk has their own way. You may ask the Master Spiritual those same questions when you finally meet him."

"And when will that be?"

"Soon," Tanto said, lowering his eyes.

"How soon?" Noke demanded.

"Sooner than you think," came a third, unfamiliar voice.

Tanto glanced up, then immediately fell to the floor, pressing his head to the ground in a bow. "Master Spiritual. I honor you."

Noke glanced up as a figure came through the doorway. He was short, but not so far from average height to make it worthy of comment. His head was polished bald and seemed to shine like a fresh-washed plate where the light hit it. He walked with a slight slouch and dry-washed his palms as though pleading for forgiveness with each step. Noke met his eyes and felt a sliver of fear curl at the back of her neck. For such a normal, unremarkable man, he had haunting eyes.

"So you are the infamous Nokemono," said the man.

Noke could only nod dumbly, arrested by the deep, alluring blackness of the man's eyes. She felt as though he could look directly into her mind and read her thoughts with those eyes. All the bullish bravado she had crept out through the back door and sprinted away. It was one thing to know when someone was stronger than you, quite another to know when someone was far stranger.

The man laughed. "Don't mind me. I know I might seem a little strange to you, but soon I won't startle you at all."

The comment only made Noke more convinced that he could read her mind, and she lowered her head as though to protect her brain from his inspection.

"My name is Daishin. Master Spiritual of this temple."

Noke could only stare until Tanto cleared his throat and muttered. "Say something."

Noke coughed and cleared her throat. "I am glad to meet you, Master Spiritual."

The Master Spiritual raised an eyebrow. "Are you truly? Glad?"

Noke lowered her chin even more and narrowed her shoulders. "I think so."

The Master Spiritual gave her a studying look.

Tanto straightened. "I have never seen her afraid," he said.

The Master Spiritual shook his head. "Oh, she is not afraid. Far from it. She is hiding."

"From you?" Tanto asked.

"From herself."

That made Noke straightened. "I am not hiding from anyone," she snapped.

Tanto smiled. "There she is."

The Master Spiritual narrowed his eyes. "I understand you wish to wield the Wind of Death."

Noke nodded. "Yes, I do."

"Is there someone you wish to protect? Some vengeance you wish to exact? What would make a young girl want to hold such a weapon?"

Noke shrugged easily. "I know it belongs in my hands. I will figure out why later."

The Master Spiritual's eyes widened and he leaned closer. "Do you have any friends, Nokemono?"

Noke thought of Hinadori and his abandonment at the Bushido Academy. She gritted her teeth. "No."

The Master Spiritual licked his teeth. "We all need friends, Nokemono. I hope you will find some while you are here."

"Will it help me get to the sword?"

The Master Spiritual smiled. "Oh, absolutely."

"When will training begin?"

"Your training has already begun. We have worked on your body for a fortnight. Resetting your bones, putting you back together. Altogether, you will be stronger in the broken places."

Noke didn't need to see proof to know that was true. Lying in that bed mat, she had never felt stronger in her entire life. If they had asked her to touch the ceiling, she could have done it in a single bound – such was the coiled power in her legs.

"Tomorrow you will become a true apprentice of the temple. It will not be easy. You are an outsider and a girl. Most of your contemporaries are boys who have grown up in this temple. They heard what you did and said to their comrade in your testing, too. They will compensate you for that."

Noke shrugged. "So be it."

"I look forward to seeing what becomes of you, Nokemono. I cannot tell if you will bring glory or destruction, but I know that whatever it is, this temple will never be the same after it."

Tanto shifted uneasily at that and glanced down at Nokemono with a look of concern.

"I have a question," Nokemono said.

"Go on."

"If I am to become a monk, will I be less of *myself*?"

The Master Spiritual touched his chin. "What do you mean?"

"Tanto said I must not question tradition, but I question everything. Does that mean I will not be welcome here?"

The Master Spiritual smiled. "I once was just like you, questioning everything."

"And what made you stop?"

His smile widened. "I still question everything. Half the conclave does not want you here and maybe they are right – but that specific question is one I would like to see the answer to."

The Master Spiritual turned to leave the room and leaned towards Tanto. "Have her readied to join the others tomorrow. We will know soon enough if she is a mistake," he hesitated, "or a miracle."

Then the Master Spiritual whispered something into Tanto's ear, and the tall monk gave Noke an absolutely devious look.

CHAPTER TEN

Noke rolled her shoulders and tilted her neck both ways, like a fighter would before a bout. The pain was still there, but she felt strength too. A new power, more potent than any she'd had before.

"New beginnings are often disguised as painful endings," Tanto said, looking her up and down.

Noke smiled. "Oh, I know all about painful endings."

Tanto slid a door open and raised his chin. "I'm sure you do."

She glanced through the door. A staircase lay ahead, dark and barely illuminated by a flickering lantern light just below. Noke sucked in a breath. There was something outlandish and mystical in the air that she could not quite figure out.

"Afraid?" Tanto asked.

"No," Noke snapped.

Tanto sighed. "When you refuse to acknowledge your fear, it moves into your shadow and does more dangerous work. It is better to admit that you are afraid and face it than to let it rule you while you run."

"I am not afraid," Noke insisted, stepping onto the staircase.

Tanto narrowed his eyes. "Go on then."

As she strode down the stairs, an eerie quiet fell upon them and Noke got the sense that she wasn't just walking down to a lower floor; she was descending into a place weirder and more unpredictable than the one above.

As though to confirm her suspicion, a sharp bark of laughter sounded just ahead and Noke gave a start, clutching her chest, as her heart thumped against her ribs.

Tanto raised an eyebrow. "I thought you were not afraid."

Noke grimaced. "Startled, that's all."

Tanto nodded in acceptance and offered his hand. Noke glared at it for a long moment before refusing. *I will not hold his hand like a little girl.*

She came at last to the end of the staircase and a large, wooden double-door with strange inscriptions along the face. Noke stared at the patterns on the wood for a while, trying to find meaning in the lines and languages she couldn't understand. There were voices on the other side of the door, a lot of them. If she had to guess, she would assume there were dozens of people beyond the door.

Noke glanced at Tanto. "Should I open it?"

Tanto nodded once. "Yes."

Noke drew in a breath and pushed the door open.

It was a large room, spotlighted by hanging lanterns, that left corners of darkness around the chamber. A dozen or more young boys sat across three wooden benches arranged in a line at the center of the room. If Noke had to judge their ages, she would say they were about her age. Fifteen, maybe sixteen or seventeen at the most. Some had the bodies of full-grown men, thick with muscle and jaws sculpted from stone. Others were still in the clutches of boyhood, with long, spindly limbs and barely their muffs of hair on their chin.

There wasn't a single girl amongst them. In fact, Noke had to think back to Akari for the last time she had seen a woman. This was an isolating place for a girl.

She noticed a tall boy sitting apart from the rest of them. Unlike the others, his white kimono was splotched with yellow and he stared at Nokemono with a look of pure animal hatred. She gave a start as she noticed that his hand was tied to his neck, such that it looked like he was trying to strangle himself. It was the boy they had brought to her test, the dopey looking one. Plainly he had been made to suffer some punishment for trying to kill her. From the look on his face, it was plain he wanted to finish the job.

Tanto cleared his throat. "Rise students."

At his command, every single one boy rose to their feet. They did it with an almost perfect synchronicity. As though they had gone through the routine of standing as one a hundred times that day. It reminded Noke in some ways of something she had seen before – a squadron of soldiers who had once paid a visit to the market. She remembered how they seemed to move as one, even when they went to different market stalls. – there was a common cadence to their movement. *Training.*

One of the boys - a big, thick-shouldered one with a deep scar across his eye - raised an eyebrow at her and stifled a laugh. He elbowed a sharp-nosed boy beside him, who also fought back a giggle.

"This is Nokemono," Tanto announced. "She is to join you all now. Give her a befitting welcome. Treat her no better or worse than you would any other student."

That made the big, scar-faced boy smile and his sharp-nosed companion finally let out a deep dribble of laughter. It caught like wildfire and soon all the boys were laughing. Some doubled over and slapped their knees as if this was a practical joke so funny and absurd as a girl monk could ever be allowed.

Noke's jaw hardened in a frown as she endured their laughter, taking it in, memorizing each smug, laughing face.

Tanto let them have their fun for a long moment before raising his voice. "Enough."

The silence came almost instantly, and the laughter cut off like someone had grabbed each one of them by the throat.

"Minato, Sora," Tanto said, staring at two boys. "Since you find her presence here so funny, I am leaving her in your charge. Make sure she gets up to our speed."

The scar-faced boy's face shapeshifted from a smiling one to a sour one.

"Master, why was I chosen?" he asked. "Sora, laughed first."

"You led him to the laughter Minato and you will lead Nokemono to know what is so funny, too."

The scar-faced boy wilted and bowed his head. "Yes, master."

Tanto straightened. "That will be all. Take her back to your dormitory."

With that, the boys filed out of the room. Noke glanced up at the scar-faced boy, Minato and his companion Sora, who had started the chorus of laughter at her arrival. A part of her wanted to slap the stupid smirks off their faces, but she knew that would not be wise. Minato looked like he could fight a bear and win. Sora had the sharp, serpentine movement of a skillful fighter, too.

Minato threaded a hand through his dark locks of hair as he glanced down at Noke. He seemed a little unsure of how to deal with a girl his age.

He spoke in a low mumble. "I…Uh…I,"

"What Min means to say," Sora interjected, "is welcome to the Shugendo monastery."

Sora waited for her response, but Noke merely blinked and said nothing. Her stare was one of pure malice.

Sora cleared his throat. "I see, not the talkative type. Don't worry, that will change – I am told I am very charming."

"Who told you that?" Minato asked.

Sora shot him an irritated look. "Loads of people."

"Like who?"

"People you don't know."

"Like – ?"

"Just shut up Min," Sora snapped.

Minato laughed as they led Noke through the door.

Nokemono's stomach growled as they stepped into the corridor and Sora gave her a pointed look.

"Hungry?" he asked.

Starving was the more accurate term, but Noke didn't want to come across as desperate to them.

"I could eat," she admitted.

Minato smiled at that. "So could I," he said with a smile. "Food it is."

He led the way down the corridor and through a thick door with the mark of a dragon painted across it. They stepped inside and the aroma of simmering beef hit her flush in the face. Almost in reflex, she clenched her jaw, grinding her teeth a little at the hint of food.

Sora caught the expression and gestured towards a wooden bench and table. "Have a seat."

She obliged as he and Minato strode towards the kitchen at the far end of the hall where the food was being prepared. They returned with two large trays of food that made Noke's mouth droop.

Mochi rice cakes, boiled eggs, daikon radish, konjac yam, tofu, vegetable broth and an almighty cut of beef. Noke had hardly ever seen so much food in one place all at once.

She stared down at the trays with an almost childish look of wonder and amazement. The extravagant food display suggests there was a festival or celebration of some sorts.

Sora gave her a confused look. "What is it? Did you want the fish instead?" he turned to Minato. "I told you we should have brought fish."

Noke shook her head. "No, this will do."

Without waiting for an instruction, Noke sat slowly down and began eating. There was no room to stand on the ceremony. This was her one opportunity to eat like a king, and she was not going to let it go to waste. Tomorrow, for her, wasn't promised.

She ate without chopsticks, restraint or respect for man or gods. With hands, with all the savage luster of an animal in the wild. She didn't care about anything for that small moment beyond stuffing her face.

Minato and Sora watched in a stunned silence as she finished her first helping and licked the bowl.

Only when she had paused for a drink of water did she finally realize that they hadn't touched the food.

She threw a boiled egg into her mouth and bit down into the yolk. "Aren't you both eating?"

They looked at her like she really was a wild animal.

"Where did you come from, Nokemono?" Minato asked.

She stopped chewing and glanced up at him. "None of your business."

He frowned for a moment, then his eyes seemed to dim. "I don't know where you came from Nokemono," he said, raising his chin, "but you won't ever have to go hungry again."

Noke narrowed her eyes as she looked up at him. She dabbed at her chin with the back of her hand, wiping away a spot of broth. "You know nothing about me, Minato. It would be best if you keep it that way."

He leaned back from her as though physically stung by her words, then straightened in his chair. Even sitting down, he seemed to tower over her and his eyes had a deep, unbreakable concentration.

"Fine," he said, with a grim look. "Let's keep it that way."

After the eating was done, they showed her to her room. She was given a single room, across from the other boys who shared a twelve-man dormitory. In her wooden wardrobe were six pristine white kimono's which were to be worn and washed in a six-day cycle. She sat in a solemn silence before the sound of a loud metal gong broke her from the restive state.

The sound of footsteps in the corridor drew her out of the room. The other students were moving in a single file in the same direction.

Noke saw Sora pass her by and touched the cuff of his kimono. "What's going on?"

He arched an eyebrow at her. "It's time for our fighting lesson."

Noke straightened, studying the boys who strode past her. From a look of things, she was both the smallest and the weakest. They weren't just boys becoming men, but they were well trained, healthy and confident. With any luck, they wouldn't have to spar in their fighting lesson.

They all filed into a large room with domed seating around a central dais. Kasa stood at the center, flanked by Tanto. Kasa held a large burlap sack, slung over his shoulder like a homeward bound rice merchant.

The area around Kasa and Tanto was marked with a perfect circle made of chalk, giving the illusion that students had gathered to watch them fight.

The room settled into silence and Tanto glanced directly up at Noke.

Kasa strode to the center of the room. "So, you want to be monks?" he said, "You want to be masters of the martial arts, of strength, of speed," he hesitated, "of magic?" he narrowed his eyes. "Well, if that is why you have come here, you are free to go."

There was an interval of silence as no one moved or stirred in their seat.

Kasa nodded. "Good. Being a monk is about none of these things. It is about humility, discipline, character and above all else, perseverance. That is what you are here to learn above all else. We are here because we believe that a higher calling is available to those who have the heart of warriors. Our traditions are as sturdy as an evergreen oak and have been passed down for generations. With every single circle of the passing of time, our legacy grows stronger, thicker," he glanced at Noke, "it gets deeper roots."

"To be one of the Shugendo, you must first win the fight within." Kasa looked up at Tanto and lowered himself into a fighting stance. "Then you win the fight without ever swinging a weapon."

Tanto, the bigger man by far, lowered into his own fighting stance and narrowed his eyes.

Kasa beckoned him forward. "Come."

Tanto smiled and then he lunged at Kasa. Noke's eyes bulged. *They are going to fight.*

CHAPTER ELEVEN

Kasa moved at the last moment, sidestepping Tanto's lunge. It was a simple, effortless movement. Like the choreographed work of a master dancer. It wasn't that Kasa was quick – that was an over-simplification. It was that he was perfect. He moved as though at a different cadence. When Tanto came for him, he moved just out of reach – an inch at the most. Never over-extending, never leaving himself exposed. When he countered, it was with terrifying precision and merciless poise. He struck the places you couldn't guard with speed you couldn't match.

Tanto stepped forward and launched a fist. It came just short of Kasa's throat and the older man grabbed him by the wrist and turned it over. Tanto winced as his wrist made a clicking sound, but he turned at the same time to twist his hand from Kasa's grip. Kasa hardly skipped a beat. He kicked out, creating a distance between them. Tanto backtracked but ended up precisely where Kasa wanted him, for he lunged forward and caught Tanto with a flying knee.

Tanto wiped a thin line of blood from his mouth and smiled. "Do not hold back, sensei."

Kasa grinned. "You asked for it."

When the fighting had first begun, Nokemono had reasoned that she had never seen two people move so fast. Now the pair quickened to a speed so bewildering that their bodies seemed to blur as they moved.

Kasa lashed out with a flurry of hands, striking hard and fast. Tanto was no slouch to fighting. He dodged and parried and blocked, doing his best not to cede ground to Kasa, who was pressing him desperately into the smallest part of their fighting circle.

"You are better than this," Kasa snarled. "Show these students."

Noke couldn't tell, but she thought she noticed Tanto narrow his eyes at that. He swung his leg in a wide circle, brought his other leg in a roundhouse to finish the move. Kasa dodged, but was nearly caught.

"Better," Kasa said. "But you're faster than this."

Tanto quickened his speed further still and that was when Noke knew she was watching something more than just two men. There was something more to them. Something magical.

It was a wonder to watch. A demonstration of pure power and honed skill. This wasn't just fighting – it was violence made art. When Tanto thought he had Kasa in a bind, the older man found a way into the hand span of space that allowed him to escape. When Tanto was on the back foot, out of desperation, he pirouetted out of danger. Kasa was the more experienced fighter, Tanto was the stronger and faster one. They danced around each other in majestic speed as Nokemono could only stare with her mouth wide open. If that was what it took to become a warrior monk, she wondered how she could ever manage it. *How will I ever get that good?*

Kasa got caught with a spinning back-fist and for the first time, Tanto had drawn blood. He raised his chin to slow the bleeding and smiled.

Before Tanto could set his feet, Kasa moved with such uncompromising speed that Noke feared he would cut right through Tanto. To Noke's surprise, Tanto's anticipation of the movement and moved just to the side – that was when Kasa threw an elbow out with such startling accuracy that it became obvious what had happened. It was a feint, a bluff. A move to get Tanto out of balance. Tanto didn't see the attack coming and got caught flush in the face. He squeezed his nostrils immediately, anticipating the nosebleed as he backed away from the circle.

Kasa let out an exasperated breath. "Well fought Tanto."

Tanto doubled over, panting. "You took it easy on me."

Kasa shook his head. "I would never do that. I respect you too much."

Tanto straightened and smiled as the blood dripped down from his lip.

Kasa turned back to the class. "That was a small taste, a raindrop in the ocean of our way."

Noke swallowed and leaned back. Her heart was thumping in her chest at the exultation in fighting skill. She was utterly blown away.

Kasa met her eye. "What did you see when you were watching us?"

Noke blinked. "Speed."

Kasa frowned. "What else?"

"Power."

He shook his head with a dash of irritation. "What else?"

Noke touched her chin. "Magic."

Kasa narrowed his eyes. "Better." He turned back to the class and spread his arms wide. "Magic is a small word. Magic is what you find in a traveling market. Theatricality and misdirection. This is something more, ancient power that is not found in just any hands."

Noke remembered watching Akari fight the Red Hand Gang. *She had it too.*

"Teach us," someone shouted.

Kasa smiled at Tanto and the younger man moved forward. "Pushups," he announced, "one thousand of them."

A collective groan sounded from the students as they all dropped into position.

"It doesn't count until the last student completes their push up," Kasa clarified.

A few students gave Noke a skeptical look at that. They expected her to let them down. She gritted her teeth as she placed her palms on the floor. *I won't let them down.*

But of course, it is easier to say and believe a thing than it is to do and achieve a thing. After Kasa had counted forty push-ups, she found the strength in her arms beginning to wane.

"Forty-One," Tanto called out.

Noke dropped and pushed back up, her arms shaking as she did. By an act of sheer will and determination, she managed sixty-seven, before her arms gave out altogether. Shamefully, she had been the first to drop.

Tanto opened his mouth to call out the next number, then paused when he saw she had dropped. "Catch your breath, gather your strength and go again."

Noke tasted metal in her mouth and her arms felt like they would snap if she managed another push up. All the same, she set her palms again and pushed to sixty-eight, then sixty-nine and at last, seventy.

The other boys looked at her with bitter disappointment. Tanto gave her an appraising look and saw that she wouldn't get up again.

"That will be all for today," Tanto said. "You are not ready to spar until you can all complete one thousand push-ups."

"That's not fair," Sora said. "Why must we all suffer because she is weak?"

Kasa lowered his voice, so deep it was barely more audible than a groan. "That is the essence of the Shugendo. To suffer on behalf of the weak. If you don't understand that, you have no business being here."

As the students were dismissed and they trailed back to their dormitories, Nokemono looked at them. Physically, they were all closer to men than boys. Every one of them looked capable of running from sunrise to sunset. Noke was smaller, weaker and skinny in all the places they were thick with muscle.

The shame she felt rumbled deep in her bones. Her weaknesses, in comparison, had been laid bare for all to see. They were leagues above her. At this rate, she would not last long among them.

That night, she caught barely a few winks of sleep. All she could think about was getting to one thousand pushups.

The next day, Noke was the first to rise. She dressed in her granted kimono and made her way to the dining hall to get an early breakfast. Thereafter, she spent an hour stretching.

Elongating and flexing her limbs, preparing for the day to come. She was convinced, this time she would get to one thousand push-ups.

To her credit, when the time came, Noke managed eighty-nine push-ups before her body surrendered. The next day, she hit ninety-three. By the end of the week, she could touch one hundred but even then, only sporadically.

She needed more. She needed to be better.

Nokemono practiced as soon as she was awake. Before sunrise, she would sneak into the domed classroom to practice her push-ups in the sand. After a fortnight, she had cracked one hundred and fifty push-ups. Still a long way from one thousand, but the improvement was clear.

It was nearing the first month when something peculiar happened. One of the other students collapsed before her. Though it meant their lesson was over for the day – Nokemono grinned. *I am not the least anymore.*

The next day, she wasn't alone in the classroom. The boy who had fallen was at her side, practicing.

On the day they all cracked two hundred pushups, Kasa seemed to hesitate before dismissing them all. Noke's arms were almost always aching, but she grew to love that aching pain as small lumps of muscle settled along her upper arms.

On the last day of the month, Kasa allowed them to keep going after the first student fell. A full five students fell before Noke did, leaving only the strongest boys ahead of her. Minato was one of the last to fall, but even he could not match Hiro – a brute of a boy with a chest like a mountain bull. Only Hiro made it one thousand push-ups without falling apart.

Kasa nodded in satisfaction when the exercise was complete. "Tomorrow, we start with a new rule. You only have to complete a cumulative total of ten thousand pushups. That means that if one man falls short, the others have to make good on his shortfall."

"You mean the strongest has to make up for the weakest?" Sora asked.

Kasa nodded. "Precisely."

After class that day, Minato summoned all the students together.

"I don't know about you guys, but I am good and tired of having to do push-ups every day."

"We all are," Sora confirmed.

"Good," Minato said, "so we need to make sure we succeed tomorrow. Hiro, how many push-ups do you think you can give us?"

Hiro touched his chin, which already had a thick flannel of hair and let out a breath. "A thousand and hundred," he offered, "a thousand and two hundred at the very most."

Minato nodded and touched a smaller man they called Aki on the shoulder. "That means you have to give us four hundred pushups, Aki. Do you think you can handle it?"

Aki gave a pained nod. "I will try."

They all made their commitments to what they would contribute to bring the sum of ten thousand pushups.

"I think we should eat together," Noke offered. "I have found that I perform better on the days I eat early and get a good practice session in ahead of time."

Minato nodded. "Sounds good to me."

"Before sunrise then," Noke said, "we meet in the dining hall."

They all agreed.

When the time came, they were all ready. Noke's focus was on one thing and one thing alone – hitting her magic number of four hundred and three. They started off well and maintained a healthy pace, but then disaster struck. Aki fell far earlier than expected at – two hundred and twelve push-ups. He tried to take on more but was utterly spent. It meant they had to make up nearly two hundred push-ups between themselves.

"I'll take thirty," Noke offered as they got to the two hundred and twentieth push up.

"I'll take fifteen," Sora offered.

"Fifty," Hiro said.

"Twenty-five," Minato said.

The others made their commitments, and the exercise continued. Some fell short of the amount they had pledged, but many more went above and beyond, pushing themselves to the utter limit to make sure they gave each other a fighting chance. Noke made it a grand total of four hundred and seventy before she collapsed. By then, it was plain they were going to win.

When Hiro finally completed his one thousand, two hundred and forty-first push up, an almighty cheer erupted amongst them. They had done it.

Kasa smiled and nodded approvingly. "Now, you are ready to begin."

CHAPTER TWELVE

Noke tapped impatiently on the lunchroom table. Minato and Sora sat across from her with an animated silence punctuated by whispers and gossip.

There were murmurs of conversation about the room and more than once, she knew the chatter was about her.

She stared down towards the steaming tureens of food arranged in a line at the far end of the room. It still baffled her that the students of the temple were permitted to have as many helpings of food as they liked. Initially, she made sure to have seconds at every meal, but now she rarely eats for the novelty wore off.

A group of students didn't conceal their pointed stares as they spoke in hushed tones with hands covering their mouths. Her jaw tightened as she chewed contemplatively on a small shaving of chicken.

Sora touched her shoulder. "Don't worry too much. Most of the boys are respectful."

Noke frowned at him. So that was what all the murmuring was about - they thought that she would be in danger when the time came for them to spar against one another.

She glared at Sora and gave him a questioning look. "I'm not worried…are you?"

He blinked. "Of course, I am and you should be too. Half the boys are twice your size with more muscles than you have teeth. They could hurt you really badly. They don't think you deserve to be here."

"That's not my concern. I can't worry about who thinks I deserve to be here. I just have to teach them righteous lessons when the time comes."

A smile tugged at the corner of Sora's mouth. "If you come up against anyone who can do more than five hundred pushups, surrender fast. You *will* get hurt, Noke."

Noke met his eyes. "I did not come here on the business of surrender."

Sora gave her a long, studying look then shrugged. "If you say so."

She looked across the room, studying each student, one after the other. The biggest of them was Hiro. Even while eating lunch, there was a radiating power to him. He chewed with an unspoken violence that made Noke wince. Of all the students in the temple, he would be the very worst to spar. She was sure of it.

There were others too, who she marked as dangerous. There was a tall, skinny one who they all called 'the Mantis'. Noke presumed they called him that for his straight-backed gait and his often-folded, almost raptorial hands; but there was something deadly in the boy's eyes, which made her think there could be something more to the name. Minato was another who was ahead of the others in size and strength. Any of these would be a pain to spar against.

A bell rang and the students all rose to their feet. Noke was late in standing, so it took her a moment to notice Kasa standing at the far end of the lunchroom. In either hand, he had a wooden sword. One was slung easily over his left shoulder, the other he leaned on as though a walking cane. Tanto stood behind him with arms folded and jaw set strong.

"Today your sparring begins," Kasa announced.

Some boys nodded and patted one another on the back. They were looking forward to it.

"To the fighting circle," Kasa said.

The students abandoned their half-eaten breakfast and made their way in Kasa's direction. Noke found that her heart was thumping in her chest as she followed the crowd. She passed a locked door and felt a strange flutter in her sternum. She glanced at the door and narrowed her eyes – suddenly sure of what she felt. *Kazeshini is in there. The Wind of Death.*

The urgent call of the age-old sword was so sharp and violent that Noke's toes curled up in her sandals as she stared at the door. It took a strong effort to stop herself from trying to force the door open and seize the sword.

A hand fell upon her shoulder and squeezed. "To the fighting pit, they said."

She glanced up. It was Tanto. His eyes were touched by the desperate dark of a penniless man and his jawbone protruded slightly at his cheek. Plainly, he knew what she knew. *Does the sword call out to him, too?*

He pushed her gently forward and with little effort; she followed the rest of the students.

They filed into the lesson room and stood around the edge of the fighting circle. Tanto moved to join Kasa at the center as all the students arrived.

Kasa threw one of the wooden swords into the center of the fighting circle. "Who is brave enough to pick the first sword?"

They all stood still. Then Hiro stepped casually into the circle.

"I am," Hiro said, picking the sword up.

Kasa smiled and hefted the other wooden sword, tilting his neck one way and then the other.

"Defend yourself," Kasa shouted as he darted forward.

Hiro raised his wooden sword just in time to parry Kasa's overhand blow but before he could gather his footing, Kasa had stepped behind him and swept his lead leg. Hiro hit the ground hard and Kasa touched his chest with the edge of the sword.

"Bravery is a good thing, but wisdom is better. The Shugendo do not rush into a challenge without knowing what it is all about."

Kasa leaned over Hiro and grabbed him by the collar, yanking him up to his feet. "Don't lean too hard on your front foot next time."

Hiro nodded as he bowed low. "Yes, master."

Kasa nodded his satisfaction and turned towards the class. "Hiro is brave. Who is brave enough to face him?"

No one answered. Kasa might have made quick work of Hiro, but the rest of the students were under no illusion of weakness. Hiro was cut from nothing but muscle and bone. The sort of boy who looked like he should be on a battlefield somewhere or hunting some great mythical beast in a forest. One squeeze of Hiro's biceps would be enough to humble anyone of the students.

When no one answered, Kasa smiled. "You are fast learners. You all suspect that Hiro would beat the breakfast out of you."

Hiro allowed himself a small smile at that.

Kasa held out his sword to the students, studying each young one after the other. He stopped at Noke and stepped close. "Why are you here, Nokemono?"

Noke glanced up. "Because I want to become one of the Shugendo."

Kasa raised an eyebrow. "Why?"

Noke hesitated and lowered her voice. "For the sword."

"Speak up," Kasa hissed.

Noke cleared her throat. "For the sword. Kazeshini. The Wind of Death. I will wield it one day."

The Mantis let out a splat of laughter. Others sniggered too. It was a thing of great amusement to them.

Kasa wasn't smiling. "Are you willing to work?"

Noke gave a grim nod. "Yes, I am."

"And you want the temple to give the sword to you?"

Noke narrowed her eyes. "Yes."

Kasa shook his head. "The Wind of Death is not something you can be given. It can only be taken. Demanded. As the rightful heritage of the greatest warrior in the Shugendo temple."

"So that is what I must become," Noke said, smiling.

"And you think that is possible?"

Noke smiled and nodded. "Of course, I do."

He threw the wooden sword across the room. "Prove it to me."

Noke snatched the sword out of thin air and shifted her right leg ever so slightly forward.

Kasa nodded to Hiro. "Fight."

Hiro gave him a questioning look. "There is no great test in beating a weakling woman like her. Give me someone else," Hiro pleaded.

Kasa's face was expressionless. "If you are to become one of the Shugendo, you will face people weaker than you. Just as you will face people stronger than you. In both fights, there is an honor to be found. Find the honor in this one."

Hiro frowned and looked away. "So be it."

He hefted his wooden sword and set his feet, blasting air through his nose as he turned to face Nokemono.

Noke looked up at the towering figure in front of her. Hiro was bigger, stronger, faster, more experienced, better trained, older. In short, by every conceivable measure, he was better than her.

There was wisdom, she considered, in throwing her sword to the ground in a forfeit. Let some other dope face Hiro. But she knew there would be no coming back from such a public and serpentile surrender. So, she set her feet too and gritted her teeth.

"Come at me," she said, shuffling her foot the get it deeper in the sand.

Hiro stepped forward. He didn't lunge, didn't jump, didn't run. It was just a single step – taken with such casual elegance that Noke found it more menacing than any charge could have been. Here was a man whose sole intent was to beat her down with a piece of wood. He looked at her like she was his favored dancing partner and he was going to ask her for a turn.

His voice was low as he stepped forward. "Are you sure you want to do this?"

Noke took her own step forward and hissed. "Of course, I am."

After that, the time for stepping was over. She shot forward with her blade raised at an angle in a maneuver that was like to cause someone serious harm.

Hiro raised an eyebrow and made a low grunt of disapproval as Noke charged forward. Just as the hilt of her sword was making its slow way into a swipe, Hiro slapped out with his own sword. Their wood clashed and she felt the first taste of his fearsome power. He was stronger, far stronger than she expected. She whirled and tried to catch him unawares with a backhand swipe. He was wise to it and parried with the irritated ease of a goat herder swatting away a fly. She struck again with all available violence, and Hiro responded in kind with an aggressive parry. The force of it was so hard that Noke's blade spun from her grip.

Hiro looked at Tanto and arched an eyebrow. "She is no match for me."

Tanto met his gaze. "Then end the bout."

Noke struggled to her feet and picked her sword back up, readying herself. She was no match for Hiro, but she would not be made a mockery of.

Hiro narrowed his eyes and flew forward with his blade hip high. Noke raised her sword to block, but he changed the angle of the attack and caught her at the side of the stomach. She heaved in a frantic breath just as half the wind was knocked out of her. She dropped to a knee, trying to gather herself, and Hiro lashed out with his wooden sword.

Hiro raised his sword. "Surrender," he urged.

Noke never would. She was prepared to lose a fight but not her pride along with it.

Hiro struck out with the sword. Blurry vision ensued as the first hit landed on the side of her head. The second hit her lower spine, bringing her to her knees. The third hit sent her to the ground, with blood drooling out from the side of her mouth.

He hefted the sword again. "Surrender."

Noke gritted her teeth. "Not today."

He brought his sword down. Noke raised her hand to block the hit and the wood crashed down, breaking her wrist.

She let out a sharp, high-pitched squeal as pain rushed up her elbow.

Hiro stood over her, satisfied with the quick work of Noke. Her hand dangled limp from her broken wrist. The pain was unbearable.

"You broke my wrist."

Hiro nodded. "You won't choose to surrender. So, I made the choice for you."

Noke picked the sword up with her other hand and set her feet again. Her heart was pounding in her chest as though fit to explode. All good sense had left her – all that was left was the fighter's high. Total surrender to violence and acceptance of the consequences. Live or die, she would make a stand. "End it if you can."

Hiro arched an eyebrow. "You're insane."

Noke stabbed at him with the sword and he stepped back out of range. Narrowing his eyes, he raised his sword. "I'll end it then."

She moved to slash at him and he retorted with a violent backhand. His sword hit her shin and something snapped. She yelped as she tilted over and pain unimaginable exploded in her leg. A small blotch of blood appeared from the hem of her kimono. Broken wrist, now a possible broken leg.

She sucked in a ragged breath and tried to stand again. Hiro fixed his stance, ready.

"Enough," came Kasa's voice as he stepped between them. "Victory by incapacitation."

He raised Hiro's hand, declaring him the victor.

Noke tried to get to one knee, but Kasa struck out with his elbow, sending her to the floor.

"It is over Nokemono. You are done fighting today."

Some of the other boys started laughing behind her as she shimmied on her back like an upturned tortoise.

Noke turned away from them, with her sword still in hand. She lowered her voice so no one else could hear. "I'll never be done fighting."

CHAPTER THIRTEEN

The leg wasn't broken, but it still was two weeks before Noke could spar again. The monks had their secret ways of healing. However, Noke still felt pain when she held a sword for too long in her right hand. Before long, she took to using her wrong hand to ease the pain.

Sparring was a procession of nightmares. Everyone beat the snot out of her. The first time someone targeted her broken wrist, he was suspended from the Shugendo for fighting without honor. That was a small help, but it did little to change the fact that she wasn't able to beat a single one of the other fighters. Not only did they have obvious physical advantages over her, they also had spent years learning and mastering all the sword forms. They had years and years of fighting choreography under their power of instant recall. No matter how often she practiced the forms, she couldn't narrow that gap.

The closest thing she had to friends were Minato and Sora, but even they stayed around her more out of obligation than sincere interest. She had been put in their charge and the monks were dutiful without hesitation.

The worst of it was when she had to fight Kenji – the dopey one she had faced in her test. Kenji still wore the scars of humiliation from their testing and when he looked at Noke, it was with pure, festering hate. If she was paired with him for sparring, she knew that a trip to the healing room would follow soon after. He was disciplined, strong and merciless. With every attack, he added a little extra to deepen her pain. Leaned his weight on her, left his elbow out to clip her nose as he turned through the sword forms. It was horrible.

One day after Kenji had drawn blood in sparring, she considered what had once seemed impossible – surrender. There was a long, stretched out moment when the entire room was silent when she took her time getting up. Then she drew in a pained breath and rose again. She could almost feel their disappointment. They were rooting against her.

The next day, she found it harder to get out of bed than any day before and when she arrived in the lunchroom for breakfast; she saw faces fall. As she loaded her bowl with eggs, tsukemono and rice, she overheard one boy whisper ahead of her – plainly unaware she was that close.

"Fine then, two months — double or nothing."

It took her a moment to realize what that meant. They were betting on when she would give up.

She walked alone to the corner of the lunchroom, sat away from the others. Minato and Sora left their own table to slide in and sit beside her. She glanced up at them.

"Good morning Nokemono," Minato said.

Noke nodded her greeting. "Did you bet too?"

Minato raised an eyebrow. "Excuse me?"

"Did you place a bet too?" she clarified. "On when I would give up."

Minato lowered his eyes in shame but tightened his lips. "I almost did – but no."

Noke nodded and turned to Sora. "Did you?"

Sora frowned at Minato. "Minato convinced me not to. Said we wouldn't be good friends if we were rooting for you to fail."

The word hit Noke's ear hard. *Friends.* Was that what Sora and Minato thought they were to her?

The torrent of emotion hit her with such unexpected force that she didn't realize what was happening until her eyes grew blurry and her lip quivered.

Minato narrowed his eyes. "Nokemono are you.... crying?"

Noke sniffed hard, wiped her tears and frowned. "Yes, I am. Is there a problem with that?"

Minato and Sora looked at each other, then both shook their heads at the same time. "No."

Noke nodded. "Good."

They ate in silence, but in that small, quiet moment, Noke knew that something had changed between them. They had crossed a barrier in that indeterminate journey from foreigners to friends.

When the eating was done, she touched Sora's arm to get his attention. "Do you think," she hesitated, "do you think teach me the forms after our lessons?"

He gave her a puzzled look. "Why?"

Noke nodded. "I need more practice than I currently have. I need to be much better."

Sora smiled. "Well, that is certainly true."

Noke raised her chin. "Your forms are probably the tidiest I have seen. You can make a dance of it. Even more than the others. I've thought about asking you before, but just…" she didn't finish the sentence.

Sora gave her a considered look and glanced up at Minato, who gave him an approving nod. He straightened in his seat and rubbed his chin. "After dinner then, before calligraphy."

Noke nodded. "Thank you."

Minato said nothing, but Noke could see from the corner of his mouth that he was suppressing a smile. *Maybe they aren't here purely out of obligation.*

An enormous bulk of a man brushed past and Noke glanced up. It was Hiro carrying an almighty helping of tsukemono. Their eyes met as he passed by. He nodded at her – almost a gesture of respect.

All of it heartened her. She wasn't as despised as she had first thought. Yes – she was far from welcome. But like everyone else, she had supporters and detractors. As she chewed her tsukomeno, she recommitted herself to the cause. *I will never give up.*

When they arrived in the fighting circle for sparring, Kasa seemed in particularly good spirits. He beamed at everyone as they came in and seemed to walk with an almost enervated sense of delight.

"Welcome students," he announced when they had all filed in. "This is the beginning of the end for some of you."

Noke arched an eyebrow and inclined her head to listen more closely.

"The Masters have determined that only five of you will become Shugendo," Kasa said.

The class exploded in murmurs as people took in the implication of that statement. There were thirteen of them in all. It meant that eight of them would not go on with a goal they had all worked so hard for. Some – like Hiro – seemed unperturbed by this revelation. Others, like Sora, seemed distressed.

"Just five?" Minato asked, "but there are thirteen of us."

Kasa nodded. "Only the best five will be taken to the next level. Six months from now, we will hold a tournament to determine who the final five will be. In the weeks to come, if we feel your values do not align with the Shugendo, we will cull you from the wheat."

Noke swallowed hard. Of the thirteen trainees she was easily the weakest, the least skilled and with her still healing leg, the slowest. She would be the betting favorite to be the first to be cut. The thought of it made her heart pound hard in her chest as looked around. She had to make it to the tournament if she wanted to stand any chance of becoming a full Shugendo.

Kenji leaned in close to whisper in her ear. "Time's up."

"For any among you who wish to take extra lessons. Tanto and I will be happy to take any trainees for an early training session before sunrise every day. This is not mandatory. If you are interested, meet us at the lunch room tomorrow."

Noke's jaw tightened. She would be there. She could accept, in her own small way, that the other boys were faster than her, stronger, better trained. But not one of them could match her resilience. *Not one.* They ate to their satisfaction every day, without any restrictions. Losing everything they owned without getting it back was never a worry for them. They didn't know the taste of roasted rat. Whatever gap there was between herself and the other trainees she would do everything in her power to close it.

She was the first to arrive in the lunchroom for the early session the next day. Before Kasa, before Tanto, before any of the boys. She took her time to practice the forms as she waited. She was halfway through a defensive shape they called the 'Leaning Tree' when a voice sounded behind her.

"You should push your front foot out a little."

She glanced over her shoulder. It was Tanto, with a basket of wooden swords heaped on his shoulder.

Noke pushed her foot forward a little, just as he instructed.

Tanto nodded his satisfaction. "You are smaller than the other fighters. In a sword fight, taller opponents can chop down on you. You want to negate this advantage by staying at an angle but fighting on the inside so they can't use their superior reach." He shifted to change her positioning slightly. "This way you can be the aggressor and use your footwork to get away when your opponent presses."

Noke moved around with the form and found that Tanto was correct. It felt more natural.

"Thank you," she said.

He nodded and smiled. "The advantage of being the first to come."

They ran through the adjusted form at least half a dozen times before Sora arrived, then Kasa and others after that.

Only six other trainees showed up for the early session – Sora, Minato, the Mantis, Kenji, Aki and Hiro. Everyone but Kasa was surprised to see Hiro there. Serious injury seemed the only thing that could stand in the way of Hiro becoming one of the Shugendo. He had everything – speed, size, strength. Even a good heart.

"Welcome all," Kasa said when the sun's light shined upon his face. "I suppose you are wondering what our first lesson will entail?"

Some nodded their agreement.

Kasa smiled. "First, we are running to the top of that hill."

He was pointing through the window at a high rising hill in near distance to the village.

There was a collective groan of displeasure. Noke felt her stomach drop. Though her leg was largely healed, running uphill would be, she knew, an exercise in agony. She said nothing and when the time came to run; she ran.

The climb was more difficult than she had expected and she spent most of it alone as all the others raced ahead of her. She finished long after the others had with a kimono sticky with sweat.

Kasa had them spar after that and Noke was paired up with Aki. Though Aki was the smallest of them, he was mean as a snake with the wooden sword in his hand and he wasted no time in getting to his work. He rushed Noke as soon as Kasa gave the opening call. Noke recalled Tanto's words about the

Leaning Tree defensive style. How it would benefit her to lean into the stance more to reduce the impact of her limited reach. It helped tremendously.

Though Aki could beat her, it was at the expense of tremendous effort and pain. Noke could feel it in her stomach – she would beat him if they sparred again. She had his measure.

After that, she watched every fight with proper attention. She picked things up as she watched and saw patterns – just as she did when she used to watch the market. The side each boy favored. Their tendencies when faced with aggression. Their resistance to pain. It was like she had finally found a secret which only revealed itself when she watching a fight – she could see each person for what they were.

That was the beginning of a new transformation in Nokemono. She began associating fighting as an art form – something from which she could create her own pictures. The forms were a good basis for combat, but like painting; they were subject to interpretation and creativity. She began combining the things she learned with all her education from being a street rat in the market. She learned to follow up the 'Tiger claw' stance with a subtle scratch with her free hand and how to kick out whenever she used the 'Leaning tree' to retreat. It was like mixing sugar and lime; bitterness with sweetness.

With every day of extra practice, she got better. She saw things with fresh eyes. If she was going to become one of the Shugendo, she would do it in her own way.

Days later, when students arrived for sparring, Kasa sat cross-legged in the sand without swords. His eyes were closed, and he didn't look up as they filed in. They stood in silent for a moment as they watched him, his head bowed in meditation.

His voice came suddenly as the first crow of the cockerel and Noke gave a start.

"You have all learned the beginning lessons of fighting. That is good, but it is only a small part of the Shugendo. There is a larger part. A more important one," his eyes snapped open, "the part of magic."

With that, he rose to his stamped hard against the sand. There was a reverberation of invisible power and the sand seemed to scatter as his foot landed. "In five months, you will face off in your last tournament and on that day, you will show all the parts of Shugendo. Today, you will learn what it means to call the rain and be sure that it will answer."

To begin his demonstration, he whispered something under his breath and raised a hand to the sky. A cloud groaned overhead and a gargle of thunder sounded above.

Kasa's face was stern as stone as he glanced up at the ceiling.

He muttered one effortlessly whispered word. "Fall."

And the rain fell.

CHAPTER FOURTEEN

As the rain fell, Kasa drew a line across the sand with his heel. He turned to face the trainees and smiled. "There is a duality to all things. This is something you must understand as Shugendo. The temporal and the spiritual. The soul and the substance." His eyes fell on Noke. "The parent and the child."

Noke arched an eyebrow. "What does that mean?"

Kasa cleared his throat. "It means that every force has an opposite and interconnected force. In all sadness, there is a bit of happiness. In all pain, there is a little joy." He pointed at the uneven line in the sand. "On one side of this line is the temporal and the other is the spiritual," he said.

Most nodded their understanding as he spoke.

He drew small crosses along the jagged line. "There are of course, intersections. Tunnels, if you will. Places in which the temporal intersects with the spiritual. We call them magic wells." He cleared his throat and bore himself up to his full height. "This is where we draw our power from. This temple sits above a magic well. It is in the air here. When the Shugendo travel, we never stray far from what magic wells. Magic is simply a power that leaks into the world. It is always there whether we like it or not but only the Shugendo have learned how to use it."

"How?" Sora called out.

Kasa stiffened. "It is like any artistic skill. It requires vision. In the same way the potter turns clay into a chalice, we muster power from the earth and turn it into something new. The mundane into the miraculous."

With that, he raised his hands, crouching low as he moved his palms in small circles. "A long time ago, there was a woman called Kimora. Now Kimora was beloved, for she was agreeable with all mankind, but what the world did not know about her was that she was born of the spiritual world – not the temporal." Kasa's hands moved faster as he spoke. "Kimora longed to return to the spiritual world, for only there could she be fully herself. So, she enlisted the help of a young adventurer who promised to take her to the spiritual world if she taught him a little magic." Kasa raised his hands high. "So, Kimora journeyed with the young adventurer for five years and taught him all the parts of magic as they searched for a gateway to the spiritual world. And it came to be that they fell in love. For they were much alike in bravery and agreeableness. When at last they found a crossing into the spiritual world, Kimora was grieved, for she did not know when she would return. And so they went about putting crossings about the face of the earth such that whenever the young adventurer was in trouble, she would return to stand by his side. But of course, magic is meant to be sealed away from the temporal world and with each passing day, the crossings go wider and magic seeps into the world."

"What is his name?" Noke asked, "the young adventurer?"

Kasa smiled at that and then spread his arms out wide. Coalescing from nothingness was a small, dancing ball of fire in his hand. "His name was Kensuke. He is the very first Master Spiritual. Father of the Samurai and the one who built this temple."

Noke's eyes widened. "Samurai?"

Kasa waved her thought away and his voice got low. "Repeat after me, wtashi no senzo no kami. Watashitachi no tsumi o yurushi kudasai."

They repeated it and Noke to felt a subtle bubble of power rising at the base of her throat.

The fire in Kasa's hand winked out suddenly as it had come. Some trainees gasped; others were stunned by silence.

Kasa glanced at them and smiled, pulling his hands back as the fire winked out. "There is a special choreography to it. A dance to draw the magic from around yourself, then you must coordinate it with your mind to make things take shape.

You can be stronger or faster than any normal man. You can set fire to an oak tree without flame. It takes focus, oneness of mind, and recitation of the eight verses of access. You are all here because we believe you might have the potential to draw from the well of magic."

Their task for that afternoon was to sit in silence for an hour before sparring and try to feel the energy around them as they recited the eight verses of access.

Kasa explained that everything in the world has a voice. The sea, the air, the earth. To hear that voice, they had to listen, and that required deep concentration.

Without the aid of the Jidakippo poppy, Noke found herself unable to concentrate. Every time she tried to commit the verses of access to memory, she failed miserably and had to be instructed again.

No one else had any luck doing anything magical – except for Aki, who by some miracle managed sending some beads of sand scattering. Before an hour was up, Tanto got frustrated with their progress in recitation and Kasa called it to an end. "Tomorrow, you must all be better at focusing your minds."

Kasa set to dividing them into pairs for a sparring session to close the lesson. To her dismay, Noke was drawn up against Kenji. There was no love lost between the pair. Kenji hated her still and she gave him all that animosity back. Of all the trainees, he was the one she didn't mind hurting. When her name was called, his lips twisted with disgust and he spat derisively at the sand – signaling his distaste.

"How many times must I beat a dog before it runs back home?" he said, loud enough for her to hear.

A few students laughed at that. Noke said nothing, letting the abuse slide off her like rainwater. Perhaps it was the effort to concentrate, or maybe it was the still reverberating magic in the air. For reasons she couldn't understand, she felt totally at peace in that moment.

When they entered the fighting circle, Noke retained the strange calm. It radiated from the sand all the way through to her wooden sword.

"This will be the day you finally learn your lesson," Kenji hissed as he snatched up his wooden sword.

Noke only shrugged. "Perhaps."

Kenji came at her with a grasping lunge and she waiting until the last moment before bringing her sword up to block his strike. Their wood clashed and she shifted sideward to avoid a second strike.

Kenji wet his lips as though about to fist as he circled her again. He was tight with coiled rage – Noke could see it in the way he hunched his shoulders up and gritted his teeth. In contrast, Noke felt free. *Like water.*

He came at her again and she spun around his attack, tapping his shoulder lightly with her sword as she did so, causing him to stumble slightly forward. She could have followed it up with a thunderclap of the sword, but she risked a counter-attack if Kenji was clever. The casual ease of it surprised even herself. At the corner of her vision, she saw the other students draw closer to watch.

"She's toying with you," the Mantis called out.

"Make her bleed," someone else cried.

Kenji snorted as he turned to face her again. The words from the crowd were getting to him. It was clear. Noke blocked out the noise, taking her mind back to Tanto's words. *Stay at an angle but fight on the inside.*

She shifted slightly to change the angle on him so he could lash out with a chopping motion that she found hard to avoid. He narrowed his eyes, circling her more slowly this time.

Noke tightened her grip on the sword. For the first time in all her fights, she felt confident. They crossed swords and broke apart and then clashed once more before Noke thumped the side of his ribs. It was a move she had coined herself. She called it 'Pickpocket'. It was a sneaky attack that made a mockery of the rigid Shugendo defense.

Kenji blew out an irritated breath as he got back into his stance. He was rattled. The blow she had dealt him was the sort that wouldn't hurt. While he was thrumming with the thrill of the fight but later, when he laid his head to rest, he would find a bruise.

To her surprise, Kenji didn't lunge into another attack. He was hesitant. She had garnered his respect and finally he thought of his next moves.

Noke gritted her teeth. It was her turn to lead the dance. She went for him, giving him no space to retreat. He was so taken aback by the outburst of aggression that his feet got tangled up as he tried to backtrack. Kenji blocked the first of her three strikes, but the second cracked him about the neck before the third sent him reeling to the floor. He made a sound like a kicked dog as his sword flew from his hand, sliding off towards the edge of the circle. This was it, her chance to be the victor. To finally prove that she belonged.

Face suddenly hot with excitement, she went at him, losing all her old calm. She brought her sword down – aiming for the shoulder but not minding if she struck the head.

Kenji raised his hand in defense and, by some combination of luck and skill, he caught her sword in his hand. He tried to snatch it from her, but she reacted just in time, pulling back so he couldn't rip it cleanly free. She kicked his elbow, and the sword came free, but momentum sent her stumbling backwards and the sword flew from her hand. She drew in a breath. It was a close call – one small miscalculation and he would have snatched her sword from her. In her eagerness, she had nearly fumbled her advantage.

She glanced over her shoulder. The sword was too far out of reach. She wasn't going to turn her back on Kenji to get it. He coughed as he tried to rise and Noke knew she had to act now. Before he could come to his full sense. It didn't matter that she had lost the sword; she didn't need one to hurt a man. Her scarred knuckles were proof enough of that.

As Kenji tried to find his feet, she struck his temple with a full-leather punch. He went down without a fight. In that moment, it was as though the gates to her rage were broken all the way open. She didn't stop punching. He tried to block the first few blows, but she was too close for him to push away. The fourth punch drew blood and when Noke drew back her fist, she felt the stinging pain of a tooth lodged in between knuckles. It didn't matter – she had been waiting a long time for this. She drew her hand back with enough intent to end it.

Someone caught her hand.

"Enough," Kasa said, "victory by incapacitation."

Heart pounding, Noke turned to face the other boys, throwing her hands up with a shout of carnal delight. "Did you see that?"

She beat her chest and stamped her foot. "How do you like me now?"

Even with her healing shin, even facing an over matched foe – she had won. *Why aren't they cheering for me?*

The boys were silent. They usually went crazy when someone won by incapacitation. Even when she was victorious, they still managed to take something from her – to withhold her praise. They wouldn't give her the glory she deserved.

"Be gracious Nokemono," Kasa said, "even in victory. That is the way of the Shugendo."

She turned to Kasa, wanting anything; his nod of approval, his raising her fist to announce her victory. He gave her nothing, too.

She threw her sword at the sand. Her heart pounded so hard that she felt it in her throat. "Gracious, you say? And what grace was given to me? Where has my grace been all these weeks?"

No one answered as Kenji was dragged away.

Kasa's face tightened in a scowl and he glared at Noke. "Control yourself, Nokemono. There is a time for stillness. If you wish to wield Kazeshini, you cannot be captive to your emotions. To draw the Wind of Death means that blood must be shed. How can you wield such a weapon when your temper is so easily set aflame?"

Noke balled up her fists, wanting for all the world in that moment to fight again, but she let out a slow breath and did as she was told. She had a victory under her belt and it would not be her last. Though no one else seemed willing to give her the praise, she was proud of herself. One way or another, she was going to be one of the five chosen to become a Shugendo. *I swear it.*

Kasa turned to the rest of them. "Your tournament lies ahead. Prepare for it if you wish to succeed. A week from now, we will have our first task. Those who fail will be sent back home."

CHAPTER FIFTEEN

The next week was the most difficult. Hours of swinging their wooden practice blades from sunrise till high noon. Then hours of loosing arrows at faraway targets with full-sized strong bows. Noke hated the bow work most of all, but she also found difficulty in finding the patience for the magic lessons which they always ended the day with. Kasa and Tanto would demand they sit in perfect silence and stillness for long periods of time until it was almost painful not to move. Then they would recite the eight verses of access and try to draw from the magical power that was supposed to be in the air. So far, sore bottoms were the only achievements Noke could show in learning to deploy magic.

On both body and brain, it was a brutal regime. All the same, Noke could feel the benefits of the brutality. She was stronger every day. Her shoulders carried a subtle hunch that spoke to the stretching skin of growing muscle. Though she had not managed to do anything magical, her mind felt like it had been sharpened to a killing point after miles and miles of silent meditation. Her sword felt better in callused hands. In the moments she wasn't sparring, she flexed her fingers, missing the weapon, trying to work out alternative forms in her mind.

With the bow, there was no match for the Mantis, who could hit any target within sixty yards – No matter how small. Sora, too, was an excellent shot. In fighting, Hiro was the clear champion, though Minato and the Mantis sometimes ran him close. With magic, no one had shown any signs of excellence, but Aki had a stillness that few could match. Noke had not proven to be exceptional in anything yet and that was an irritating truth. One good sword swing was all it would take for Hiro to send her sword spinning out of her grip. With the bow, she couldn't hit targets further than forty yards with any regularity. It was slowly becoming clear who the best trainees were, and she was not among them.

She still trained like a lunatic and was getting better every day, but it was hard to bridge the gap between herself and the very best trainees. They had simply been doing this for so much longer than she had.

When the day of the test finally arrived, she was tired, hungry, bruised and burdened. Though the tournament was still four months away, it was plain that some trainees would not participate in it. Kasa and Tanto made it clear that their aim was to whittle down the number of trainees to less than ten before the tournament.

As they enjoyed a specially appointed breakfast, Kasa and Tanto stepped into the dining hall. Kasa wore a pale white kimono, while Tanto wore a sober black one. Across his shoulder, Tanto carried a long hardwood case.

Kasa folded his arms and smiled. "It's time for your first test."

The muttering simmered down to silence as all the heads turned towards Kasa.

Kasa wet his lips. "The test of long-suffering is where we will determine who among you is truly fit to serve the Shugendo. Pack a single bag and meet me outside the temple," he ordered.

Noke narrowed her eyes as she rushed to obey. She had hardly anything to pack, save for a needle, thread, water flask, a small bread knife she had sharpened over the weeks in the temple, her bow and a small quiver of arrows. They had been told very little about what to expect, but Noke reasoned that if they were going out of the temple, it was likely they would face unexpected perils.

Outside, Kasa led them in a brief recitation of the magical verses of access and Noke found that it came easily to her. Even as she spoke, it was as though she did so from an otherworldly place and the sounds of her own voice reverberated through her mind.

Kasa gave her a satisfied look and turned towards the mountain. "At the summit of the mountain, there is a tree called the white tabunoki. It has leaves that are touched with red at the edges. Your test is simple - bring back a single leaf, plucked from the tabunoki within three days. If you do not return within three days, then you will not be admitted to the temple. The last two to return will be also be expelled from the temple."

Noke arched an eyebrow. *Sounds easy enough.* She only had to ensure she wasn't one of the last two to return. She would pass the test, she simply had to. There was nowhere else for her to go and the call of Kazeshini was still screaming at the back of her mind.

The rest of the trainees wore disappointed, worried looks as soon as Kasa had explained the test. Even Hiro looked like he had been given terrible news.

Noke leaned in to Sora and whispered a question. "Why is everyone so worried? it sounds like a straightforward test."

Sora gave her a straight look. "Have you not heard of what happens at the summit of the mountain?"

Noke shook her head. "No."

Sora raised his chin. "The Tengu reigns in the mountains."

Noke stifled a laugh. "There's no such thing as Tengu."

But Sora's face was deathly serious, with no hint of mirth.

"Are you serious?" she asked.

Sora swallowed. "Very."

Noke wasn't sure whether to believe him, but there was something in the set of his jaw. The pulsing vein at the side of his head that made her think this wasn't just a childish prank. If Tengu did truly exist and live on the mountain, then how on earth were they meant to make it back alive?

Kasa nodded towards Tanto and the big man set the hardwood case down across the floor. He unfastened a copper clasp and folded it out at the hinge.

Inside were thirteen swords, wrapped in black cloth sheathes.

Tanto held the largest one out. "Hiro."

Hiro stepped forward and bowed low, accepting the sword in two hands.

"Minato," Tanto said, holding out another sword.

Minato accepted with the same mode of deference.

The handouts continued until it came the turn of Noke; she was the last to receive a sword.

"Nokemono," Tanto said, as she stepped forward.

The sword was simple, a slightly curved, single-edged blade with a copper cross-guard and a tightly bound cloth sheathe.

A pang of stilted anxiety ran up to Noke's knee as she fastened the sword to her back. If they were giving them each a sword, it meant they expected them to need them. Thoughts of the Tengu flooded her mind as she considered the once unimaginable possibility that the creatures from storybook could truly be real.

Kasa pointed up towards the foot of the mountain, which lay only a brisk walk ahead. "From here on, you are on your own. Keep your wits about you and remember the way of the Shugendo always. If you do not return to the temple within three days, then your time with the Shugendo is over. There is no shame in that. It is to your great credit that you have come this far — there are no losers now."

Noke's heart beat faster. This was it. A real, dangerous challenge. A mountain to climb with a boon to claim at the summit. If she meant to wield Kazeshini, then this was precisely the sort of test she would have to overcome. She sucked in a breath, let it out in a slow wheeze and gritted her teeth. *Bring it on.*

"Three days," Kasa said, "Go!"

They all took off running. Noke lagged behind – climbing uphill was not her strength – but even so, she knew she could keep running longer and harder than most of the other boys. This was not a test of speed; it was a test of resilience.

She kept running and soon came to the foot of the mountain. As she ran up, she could hear the desperate drum of blood pumping in her ears.

Hiro had built up a healthy lead on the pack, but with time, she caught up to Aki and Kenji. She stared up the mountain towards Hiro who seemed fresh as when they had started. Nokemono straightened, trying to match his stride, but her energy chamber was almost completely empty. She stood no chance. Hiro was something else.

After an hour of hard running, a thick fog appeared ahead. She had overtaken at least three boys, but she could hear their heavy breathing just a few strides behind her. There were no sluggards amongst them.

The air cooled as she stepped into the fog. She sucked in a grateful breath of air. Her heart pounded like a marching drum and her lungs seemed to burn in her chest. She was blowing like a fish, but there was still power in her legs. She wasn't done yet. The fog thickened, and she had to squint to make out what was ahead of her.

She glanced back over her shoulder and noticed, for the first time since the climb had begun, that she was alone. The mountainside was quiet and through the thick fog she couldn't see anyone nearby.

"Hello?" she called out.

No answer came.

Noke licked her teeth. *When did that happen?*

She heard the faint clatter of hooves carried on the wind and gave a start. She half expected a chariot to come charging towards her, but none appeared.

Noke squinted into the fog. It was nearly impossible to make anything out. *Keep going.*

She tightened her grip around her knife and stepped into the fog. The sound came again, faint but unmistakable. *Hooves.*

The smell of something burning made her slow down to a snail's pace, but in the fog, she couldn't see the smoke, nor could she tell where the flame was coming from.

Fueled by pure grit, she kept going. Ever-so-often she called out to the others, hoping that someone would answer, but no response came.

Snap.

Noke dodged instinctively and an arrow nicked the edge of her ear as it whistled past. The sharp twang of a bowstring was a sound so familiar from the many days in practice. Hearing it had triggered an almost subconscious natural reaction. That little movement had almost certainly saved her life.

Was it an accident or an attack? She brought down her bow and nocked a single arrow, muscles tightening at the force of the draw weight as she pulled slowly back. "Who goes there? I am of the Shugendo."

Of course, it was not entirely true, but Noke thought it was worth saying. If it was one of the other boys who had loosed an arrow accidentally, then they would know the sound of her voice. If it was a stranger or an attacker, they would know to tread with caution when it came to the Shugendo. No response came.

She recited the verses of access under her breath, trying to listen. If Kasa was right and everything had a voice. Who – or what – was speaking at that moment?

She opened her mind to take in what her ears were telling her. The silence was total. No whispering wind, no singing birds, no bleating cattle. *Why is it so quiet?*

For the mountainside to be a silent could only mean one of two things – either there was nothing close enough to make a sound; or, more worryingly, everything was holding its breath.

The sudden sound of hooves came again. This time, there was no running from it. Whatever it was – it was close. She sucked in a breath and tried to find the focus in that moment. "I am no easy prey," she whispered as she released the arrow. It flew true into the fog and the silence returned.

Her sword kissed it's sheathe as she dragged it free.

"I am no easy prey," she said again, eyes narrowing as she readied herself for violence.

A faint hint of shadow preceded the jolt of movement ahead as a creature hurled itself through the fog. Noke screamed as she lashed out with the sword. Her swipe fell well short – a horrible miss. If the beast had meant to kill her, she would have been ten times dead. Panting hard, she looked up at the figure towering over her.

His dark silhouette cast her halfway in shadow. The creature's hair was an unruly tangle of white above a face cut from hard lines and sharp sinew. His nose, if it indeed it could be called that, was something akin to the beak of a bird. In one gnarled fist, he clutched a long pewter staff and in the other the twisted pieces of a broken arrow. His kimono was half white on one side and painted red on the other. Noke noticed the way it stood just to the side and knew from a single look that the creature was no stranger to killing. She took in everything about it and could conclude on that matter with only a few glances. This was no scare story. It was real.

A thing from a nightmare. A tengu.

CHAPTER SIXTEEN

It looked half like a man, but its nose was long and bird-like and its hair had the strange consistency of hanging vines. White whiskers framed its mouth and its eyes had the stillness of a porcelain doll – never seeming to move. It walked with half a limp and favored its right side. Noke noted that she could use that if it came to it. *Go for the weaker side.*

The more she was terrified, the less she could look away. All she could smell; all she could feel was the tengu's dominating presence.

Noke muttered in prayer. "Ebisu, god of fortune. Whose eyes see all hearts. Have mercy on me."

The tengu arched an eyebrow.

Noke's jaw tightened. "Omikami, creator of all. Watch over me. Hachiman, lord of battles, fight for me."

The creature exhaled through its nostrils and its breath was hot as kettle steam.

"Protective gods of my ancestors lend me your strength. Lend me your diligence."

She continued to mutter the words to herself as she glanced up.

All tengu had red skin, but this creature seemed to be of a lighter shade. Pink almost. Noke had always told herself that if she saw one in person, she would not be afraid, but now knew that was a lie. Though she didn't run, her heart pounded with the fear of flight. Every instinct screaming at her to get away but something kept her steady. Slowly, she wordlessly whispered the verses of access until she felt a bubbling sensation in her stomach.

The tengu's lips spread in a twisted smile and Noke's stomach turned sideways.

"Why aren't you running?" the tengu asked, almost mockingly.

Noke's mouth was dry as she fumbled for the words. There were many reasons she didn't run; she was tired and angry; she had nowhere to run. The compulsion to run was strong, even in the fog. There were plenty of reasons to be anywhere but there. But she knew she couldn't. It was a mantra she had made her own from the day she had first glimpsed Kazeshini. A memory of a little girl touched her mind. Sucking her thumb and refusing to eat the food given to her.

She spoke the words with grim determination. The time for running was long gone. To become the woman she wanted to be, she had to take a stand – even against the unimaginable. She almost spat the words out. "I am no easy prey."

The tengu squinted and his smile seemed to widen. Only then did Noke notice the red wetness of blood on his lips. She gasped. His kimono wasn't half red – that was blood.

Something about the sight of blood sent a hot bolt of anger from her toes up her neck. Whose blood, was it? An ambling mountain creature? One of the other trainees?

Her grip tightened on her sword. "Did you kill any of the others?"

The tengu gave a slow nod. "I did."

"Who?"

The tengu touched its chin and folded its hands in a mocking raptorial pose. Noke's heart fell. *The Mantis.*

She lowered her chin and set her feet. "Then you have a debt to repay."

She arched back into the Leaning Tree stance and raised her sword.

The tengu threw its head back and laughed. "You mean to fight me, little girl?"

She narrowed her eyes. "I mean to kill you, demon."

The tengu jerked sharply back and raised its pewter staff. It smiled and said, "Demon is a small word to what I am.

I am delivered death, the beginning of sorrow, the fabric of nightmares."

"And I am Nokemono," she replied easily

The tengu shrugged and twirled its pewter staff. "I suppose we will see if you are easy prey after all."

Noke sucked in a breath and closed her eyes for only the faintest moment, listening to the mountain, trying to hear its voice. It had nothing to say as the tengu came at her with all available force. With one swing of its pewter staff, Noke left her feet. *The power in this creature. I don't stand a chance.*

Noke felt a bruise start to purple behind her ear and knew that the tengu was far stronger than she could have imagined. It hit with a true wallop. Never in her life had she been hit with such crushing force. She readied herself for another strike as she circled the tengu, but it lashed out with startling speed. She fended off the first blow with a raised sword, but the second caught her across her stomach. Even for someone as battle-rugged as Noke, there comes a time when we all have to give up. As the tengu raised its hand for a third time, she ducked underneath and struck it with the pommel of her sword. It barely moved from the strike, offering her no sign of weakness. That thought came to her mind again. *I don't stand a chance.* As though to punctuate that thought, it brought its pewter staff down like a gavel on her forehead. It wasn't just enough to concuss someone; it was the strike of a thing that wanted to destroy her. Her vision blurred as she hit the ground and the tengu stood over triumphantly, teeth bared and muscles flaring.

She whispered as she closed her eyes. "Gods of my ancestors, led me your strength…please".

Something made Noke jerk violently. Then her eyes snapped open. She was standing again; face to face with the tengu. They locked eyes. Something about that long-extended moment of pure fear and mangled rage triggered a reaction in Noke's mind. Beneath the disguise of reality, a door in the corridors of her mind had been unlocked. She saw everything clear as day. Clear as untouched freshwater.

Something called out to Noke, clear as a bell in her ear. Not like the voice of man but that of a thing. Like the call of Kazeshini. She sucked in a breath and saw it clear – just at the edge of her vision. For the first time in her life, Noke touched a well of magic.

Power flooded her as she embraced it. It was like a bucket of water after a desperate thirst. She reveled in it for that small moment, radiating with the enervated glory of borrowed strength.

The tengu shuffled back from her, holding its pewter staff up high. "Impossible."

Noke thought it was impossible too, but here she was and here it was.

Noke flowed effortlessly into the fighting stance 'Boat Floats Along the Waters.'

The change was instantaneous. A half instance before the tengu moved, she heard the soft shift of sandal in the sand. She darted left and swiped her sword instinctively right. It connected with the tengu's pewter staff as the creature curled snake-like around the hit.

It was a purely instinctive attack, as easy and unthinking as breathing.

The tengu, momentarily shocked by the speed of her offensive, rolled in the mud to escape her chopping sword motion. Noke felt all her senses attuned to the blistering present. She was, perhaps for the first time, totally in the fight. Nokemono's nose told her the tengu sweat like a man – if it can sweat, it can bleed. Her ears told her that the creature's sandals would encumber its speed. Her eyes told her that the creature was not trained to fight. She saw it then for what it really was – a merchant in the business of fear. The moment you saw the tengu for what it really was, it no longer looked quite so terrifying.

"You will die today," Noke said easily. She meant it too. She had the measure of the tengu now.

The tengu snarled and spoke words in a language she could not understand.

She opened her mouth and a response in the same language poured out. "Marrakah bota haddan."

The tengu jerked back as though struck, then lashed out at her again. It wasn't nearly fast enough. She watched it and could almost count every footstep. She sidestepped the tengu and cut across it with the sword. Blood spattered as her sword found its mark. The tengu hissed and turned around as though offended by the cut. Before it could pirouette, Noke was inside the reach of his pewter staff, giving it no time to counter-attack. Her onslaught was vicious, intentional and laced with accrued malice. She moved as though possessed and put the sword through the tengu so quick her hand barely seemed to move. The tengu's eyes widened with shock, then its body went tense in her arms. She looked right into its face and could almost see the moment life left as the eyes went cold.

Snap!

The sound came as suddenly as the first time. A loosed arrow from somewhere out in the fog. Noke glanced up as the tengu slumped dead and the fog dissipated. A cool breeze passed over her and the magic left, leaving her body cold.

Kenji stood a few yards away with the bow and arrow in hand. Beside him stood Reshi, who was as close to Kenji's shadow as any person could be.

They stared at the body of the slumped tengu before Nokemono as Kenji lowered his bow. Reshi's eyes doubled wide.

"I can't believe it!" Reshi screamed. "You killed a tengu!"

Noke narrowed her eyes and nodded. She opened her mouth to say something modest in acceptance when Reshi shouted again.

"Kenji killed a tengu!" he shouted.

Noke gave him a confused look. "What?"

Then she noticed the arrow fletching protruding from the dead tengu's back and realized what was happening. *He thinks Kenji killed it.*

"No," Nokemono protested. "I had already killed it."

"Nonsense," Reshi spat. "I saw it with my own eyes. Kenji the demon killer."

"You think a tengu could die from a single arrow?" she asked.

He turned on her with a face of bubbling incredulity. "I'll believe that one arrow from Kenji killed a tengu before I ever believe that *you* killed one."

Noke opened her mouth again to protest but saw the futility in it. None of the boys would believe her. She could hardly believe it herself. Were it not for the dead tengu at her feet, it would have been difficult to believe what had just happened. She had summoned magi bags of it. Then killed a tengu with the magic she summoned. It was triumph to write songs about and she knew no one would give her the glory. Of all people to steal her moment – Kenji was by far the worst.

She bowed her head with resignation as Reshi started to chant 'demon killer'.

With the fog cleared, they soon found the rest of their group. Save for one – the Mantis — who had almost certainly been killed by the tengu.

Hiro quickly assumed the mantle of leadership. A role that fit him as easily as a sword fit its sheathe. When he spoke, others listened. When he walked, others followed. There was no argument about it – it just felt right.

She caught sight of Sora up ahead and gave him a gentle wave, just as Minato made his way towards her.

Minato stepped up beside her and gave her a weak smile. "Is it true what they are saying?"

Noke raised an eyebrow. "What are they saying?"

"That Kenji killed a tengu. That he saved your life."

Noke suppressed a scowl and lowered her gaze. "People believe what they want to believe."

"I knew he was lying. What really happened?"

Noke looked up at him. "Do you really want to know?"

He nodded. "I do."

She met his gaze. "I killed it. It was dead in my arms before Kenji's arrow penetrated the tengu's spine."

Minato gave her a long, appraising look and for a moment she thought he would believe her. Then his lips curled into a smile and he shook his head. "I guess I'll just have to live without knowing the truth – since everyone is telling fairy stories."

Noke shrugged and kept walking. They didn't have to believe her. She had experienced something that none of them had – magic, true, beautiful magic.

The sky darkened and Noke glanced up. They were nearing the summit but would struggle to reach it before dark. As steep as it was, it would not be prudent to keep climbing after nightfall.

The first day was over, and one trainee was dead. Spirits were low, but more than anything, they wanted to get back to the temple. She drew in a deep breath and rolled her shoulders. *Just keep going, Noke. Glory lies ahead.*

As the sun finished its shift and lowered itself to let the moon have its way, they slowed to a crawl.

"We should rest for the night," Hiro said, "find a place to sleep".

Though they all agreed, there was an apprehension to their harmonious. Though only two had seen the tengu alive. Many others had seen the corpse. The thought of sleeping in a place where tengu walked around with impunity was cut from the sort of terror that most had not known since they left the nursery. They exchanged sidelong looks and wary frowns.

"Sleep?" Sora asked. "Near the summit of the mountain? With tengu and the gods know what else skulking about?"

"We will take turns standing guard over one another, but we none of us will make it back to the temple without rest. I know it seems strange, but we have to sleep."

Sora frowned but gave no response. As frightening as it was, no one could disagree with Hiro's granite logic. He was right – if they didn't sleep tonight, they would likely die tomorrow. There was no other way.

They found the perfect location beneath a large, powerful tree with bark that seemed almost golden in the moonlight. Aki set to striking up a fire and the rest made camp.

"I'll take the first guard," Noke said.

Hiro gave her a long look, then an approving nod.

"So will I," Minato added.

"Me too," Sora said.

"Good, we have our first three guards. There are twelve of us left, so we can rotate every three hours, three guards each time."

Noke smiled. She had predicted that would be the rota and going first meant that when she slept, it would be without interruption until the morn. Tengu or no, she was far too tired to care about demons.

Minato nodded to her and hefted his sword. "First watch then, got any interesting stories?"

She smiled and he smiled back, forgetting herself. Soon as she realized how stupid she must have looked; she hastily wiped the smile from her face. "No," she spat.

CHAPTER SEVENTEEN

Cuts of roasted serow meat hung from a stick above the cookfire as the moon reached its full bloom. The rest of the trainees were asleep, but Noke, Minato and Sora were wide awake. Aki had been the one to catch the serow with an ingenious trap. Noke had been the one to have it skinned and quartered for dinner. The meat was tough but tasty and they still had enough water to wash it down well. Tomorrow, they would have to find water or face a hard trek back.

Sora tossed a scrap of gristle into the fire and it hissed and sighed.

"You skinned that serow without even batting an eye," Minato began, "not even when the blood spurted in your face. You cut it like you were cutting bread."

Noke shrugged. "So?"

Minato gave her a long look. "Who were you before you came to the temple?"

Noke arched an eyebrow. "A street rat. An eta girl."

Minato shot her a reproachful look. "Don't call yourself that."

Noke rolled her shoulders. "It's what I am. Why hide it? I know most of you are thinking about it."

Minato shook his head. "I don't think that, and neither does Sora. Isn't that right, Sora?"

Sora nodded his affirmation. "Why would anyone think that?"

Noke gave Minato a suspicious look. "Who were you before you came to the temple?"

Minato heaved in a dry, raspy breath. "My father was a blacksmith. He made an honest living working the iron and soon I worked the iron too. I was supposed to be a blacksmith like my father, making a living watching metal bend in the coal."

"Then what happened?"

Minato's face hardened. "Some bandits attacked our village. The Jade gang. My father tried to defend our home, but there were too many of them. They beat him down, used his metalwork against him." The wrinkle in Minato's nose thickened until Noke was sure his jaw would snap. She saw the veins marble around his enormous fist as he gripped his weapon.

"They killed him," Minato said at last. "Beat him to death. I tried to fight back, but I was only a boy. They took their turns beating and laughing at me. They would have gone after my mother too if the Shugendo did not arrive when they did."

Noke narrowed her eyes. "The Shugendo saved you?"

He nodded. "Yes."

"I thought they were just monks. I didn't know they ever left the temple."

"That is not the way of the Shugendo. Not everyone who becomes one of the Shugendo must stay. There must also be others who take their learning and go out into the world to proclaim the Shugendo way."

"Isn't that what the whole split within the House of Blood was about? The Master Spiritual wanted to sit in the temple meditating and the Master Temporal actually wanted to change in the world?"

Sora shook his head. "That is an oversimplification. There are special Shugendo, trained to go out into the world and exemplify the way. Called the Wayfarers."

That word "Wayfarers" hit Noke hard, like a falling boulder down the mountain, and yet it felt strangely familiar. "The Wayfarers?" she asked.

"That's right," Minato said. "The Wayfarers saved the rest of my family. The rest of our village. They got my family to safety and when I asked if they could take me in, they agreed. When I become one of the Shugendo, I will become a Wayfarer."

Sora's expression was more solemn than she had seen it before. "Me too," he said.

Noke glanced up at him. "What's your story?"

Minato inched forward and smiled. "Oh, you are going to like this one."

Noke gave him a sharp look. "Why was he a market street rat, too?"

Minato shook his head. "The opposite."

Sora looked away.

"What does he mean?" Noke asked.

Sora sucked in a tired breath and exhaled silently.

Noke touched her chin. "What's the opposite of a street rat," she looked at Sora, "son of the emperor?"

Sora squirmed and blinked.

"No," Noke said with a gasp. "The emperor is your father?"

Sora didn't look at her. "Uncle," Sora clarified, "the emperor is my uncle."

Noke's eyes widened. "Does that mean you lived in the —?"

"Palace, yes," Sora said, "with servants to attend to my every need."

Noke's mouth drooped in shock. "And you left that for this?"

He nodded. "Yes."

"Are you crazy?" Noke snapped. "Why on earth would you do something so stupid? Do you know how many people would kill to be in your position?"

"That is part of the problem," Sora hissed.

Noke arched an eyebrow. "I don't think I understand what you mean."

Sora cleared his throat. "Being the heir of one of the oldest families in the kingdom comes with a special sort of loneliness. The sort which allows you to be surrounded by people but always alone. Never knowing who just wants to use you like a rung in a ladder. I came to the Shugendo because it was a place where my past wouldn't matter. My upbringing wouldn't do me any favors. The Shugendo is a place where only hard work matters. None of my friends at the temple care who I am, they only care what I can do. I wouldn't trade that for the world. If I was back home, they would push me to marry someone I barely know – that is what it is to come from a place like me. To have a life which isn't completely your own. To be always burdened by the perception of others. It wasn't good for me – I had to get out."

"And how did you manage that?" Noke asked.

"Through a window. I wore my servant's clothes and climbed down three stories, risking death or breaking. No one knew what I looked like outside the palace walls. To them, I was just another servant going about his business. It wasn't till I made it through the city gates that I heard the sounding of the imperial gong – the alarm for everyone in the city."

"Didn't they come looking for you?"

"Not for very long. My uncle is the captain of the guard. I think he realized soon enough that me being gone was very advantageous for him."

"And why did you come to the Shugendo temple? You could have gone anywhere else."

"I was done with the games of rule. I wanted to serve. Serve something higher than myself. Something more noble."

Noke sank back, staring at the fire. "Very…noble of you both."

Minato looked at her, fire dancing in his eyes. "Why did you choose the Shugendo?"

Noke narrowed her eyes. Next to theirs, her reasoning seemed so selfish and shallow. She hadn't given up as much as Sora. Noke had no noble cause to defend like Minato.

Nokemono raised her chin. "I came for a sword," she said.

Minato blinked. "What?"

"The sword Kazeshini. It calls out to me. It is a call I cannot resist. I am born to wield that sword."

Minato's eyes widened as he gave a soft gasp. "It was you, wasn't it?"

Noke shot him a confused look.

"At our lesson one day, Tanto and Kasa ran out abruptly. It was like they sensed something was happening. The rumor was that a stranger had touched the Wind of Death."

Noke lowered her gaze.

Sora leaned forward. "That is no ordinary sword, Noke. There is magic in it that is older than this mountain. Secret spells that go back from before there was any civilization in the world. Why did you touch it?"

Noke shrugged. "I had to."

Minato touched his chin and gave Noke a long, considering look. "I have heard about that before. The call of magic. They say that magic calls out to some special people to do something significant in the world. It can be for the great good or for the great evil."

Noke arched an eyebrow. "How do you know what side is calling?"

Minato rolled his shoulders nervously and made a sign with his hands to ward away evil spirits. His eyes were darker than she had ever seen them before and he looked like a man burdened with a weight too bold to bear. He set his jaw and gave her a hard look. "No one can know what side is calling, Nokemono," he turned away, "that's why most people don't answer the call."

No one said anything else after that. Nothing needed saying. When their shift was over and they all laid their heads to rest, Noke could think only of Minato's words. *No one can know what side is calling, Nokemono.*

CHAPTER EIGHTEEN

Noke jerked awake at the sound of a shout. It was a cry of alarm.

"We're under attack!" Aki shouted.

Noke snatched her sword from the ground with pure instinct. Minato was already on his feet with his feet set to the Leaning Tree sword form. Sora was slow as ever in the rising, but he, too, was getting his grip on the world.

Half the other boys were already fighting up ahead. Hiro took on two attackers. He was bigger than both and gave them all that they were looking for. Noke squinted in the darkness to see who the attackers were.

They were men, it seemed; older than the trainees but armed with crude instruments of violence. Bandits perhaps, though it did not seem they had come to steal anything. There were more than a dozen of them, Noke was sure – perhaps double that. But the trainees were not afraid – they were of the Shugendo and that meant they stood when others would run.

Noke charged into the melee and raised her sword high.

A skinny man moved to engage her and their blades clashed. For one of the first times in her life, she was sure she was stronger than her opponent. This was not a man used to fighting. She told by the cut of his muscle and how he stood with the sword. She kicked him back and closed the distance with a defensive stance, then she lashed out with the blade battering him to a single knee. It was all too easy, and that made her suspicious.

She raised the sword and knew in that moment she could kill the man. She could see in the man's eye that he knew it, too. He lowered his weapon in wordless defeat, accepting he would die.

Noke clenched her teeth, then hesitated.

"Wait!" she called out. "These men are not fighters."

Aki slapped his sword against another man and snarled in response. "Then why are they fighting?"

"She's right," Hiro said. He had already marshaled his own opponents into a pathetic trembling circle and could have put an end to their lives if he wanted to. He lowered his weapon and held them in place with a glare. "What do you want? Why are you attacking us?"

The fighting seemed to stop as the men slunk back. "You are sleeping beneath our sacred tree," one man said.

Nokemono glanced up at the large tree. It was – she had to admit – a particularly stately and prominent tree for one on a mountain. The bark had a remarkable golden tinge to it, too, in the moonlight.

When she looked at the faces of the men, she saw them for what they were. People who felt undermined, disrespected, treating as nothing. When it came to feeling like you were treated as nothing, Noke had a bottomless experience. So, she did what she knew was the right thing. The only remedy for affronted pride.

She bowed low and pressed her head to the floor. "We are sorry."

The rest of the boys looked at her curiously, but she didn't move.

"We are sorry," Minato repeated and he too pressed his forehead to the floor.

Sora sighed as he bowed low. "We are sorry."

One by one, the rest of the trainees bowed low and gave their apology. Kenji was the last of all to apologize but loathe to be left out – he too bowed.

The men were plainly heartened by the mark of respect and supplication. They helped Noke to her feet and spoke to her as if *she* was the leader.

The tallest of them stepped forward. "Your apology is accepted. You do not know our customs and we ought to have instructed you before attacking."

He glanced down at her, then bowed low. "We are sorry."

The others followed his lead and offered their apologies in return.

In that insignificant gesture of exchanging apology, perhaps a dozen lives were saved. Noke knew the trainees would have made quick work of the men but of what worth was violence when peace was available.

"We are the people of this mountain. We protect the trees and creatures here as best we can. Forgive us for being suspicious of armed intruders. We have not been treated very well by those who come from down below. Only the ones who come from the temple respect our ways."

"We are of the Shugendo," Minato said, "we also come from the temple."

The leader gave them a studying look. "You look a little young to be of the Shugendo."

"We are trainees," Sora explained. "We are learning the ways."

The leader nodded. "I understand. Well, if you are from the temple, then you are certainly no enemies of ours."

The others agreed to and gestured their agreeance by lowering their weapons.

Noke smiled and gave a gesture of thanks to their leader.

The leader met Noke's eye. "Is there any way we can help you? We know these mountains better than anyone that walks on two feet."

Noke glanced at Hiro, then touched her chin. "We came looking for a tree," she said.

The leader gave her an appraising look. "What tree?"

Noke considered her words. What if the white tabunoki was another one of their sacred trees? Would that lead to a return to fighting? *No.* The Shugendo would not send them to pluck from a tree that was sacred to another person. That was not the Shugendo way. Patience, diligence, resilience and concentration. That was what they had been told to learn.

"The white tabunoki tree," Noke answered.

The leader touched his lip. His eyes going wide as he considered what she had said. For a moment, Noke thought that perhaps she had said the wrong thing. Then his lips curled into a smile. "The white tabunoki," he said, hesitating for a long moment. "We can take you to it."

There were many lessons Noke had learned on their test. But the hardest one which she wished she had never had to understand was thus – do not climb with mountain people; they will set a murderous pace.

The mountain people climbed with all the ease of a street cat in a cobblestoned alley. It was as though to them; the mountain had no incline and they found no struggle in walking up it.

While the trainees struggled were dripping with sweat and breathing hard, the mountain people seemed hardly moved by the climb. To them, climbing was a way of life. For an hour, without much in the way of conversation, the mountain people led the way and the ground dwellers struggled to keep up.

The leader smiled. "You are struggling, aren't you?"

Noke laughed.

Though the mountain people seemed thin to the point of skinny, they had calf muscles that were nothing but hard muscle and gristle. They were built to climb in the same way that birds were built to fly. There was no shame in not matching them.

"You will be coming here more often, if you become Shugendo," the leader explained.

"What do you mean?" Noke asked.

The leader gave her a confused look, then one of the other men laughed. "You don't know, do you?"

"Know what?"

"The monks come for the white tabunoki every morning."

Noke felt her stomach turn. *Every morning.* That was a murderous regime. Where did they find the time? Coming in three days was bad enough but every morning? How was that even possible?

"You can't be serious," Noke said.

The leader laughed. "You will see how serious I am soon enough." He jumped and gestured ahead. "Welcome to the summit, there lies the white tabonuki."

Noke looked ahead and stopped still, suspended by shock and awe at what she saw.

"Woah."

CHAPTER NINETEEN

The white tabonuki was a tall, stout, evergreen tree with bark that looked winter white in the sunlight. Noke spent a good minute just staring at it.

"Did you come all this way just to look at it?" the monk said.

Noke cleared her throat and remastered herself. "No, of course not." She stepped close and plucked a leaf from the lowest lying branch. It didn't look different from any other leaf. Entirely indistinguishable from a hundred other forest leaves, they could have plucked along the way. She stuffed her pockets with as many leaves as she could manage.

The other boys did the same, stripping the tree of half its green within minutes.

The leader of the monks laughed. "Allow the tree to keep some modesty," he said.

The boys took heed. They had gathered more than enough leaves – the hardest part of their test was done. On the way up the mountain, they had acted as though on several individual tasks - each person trying to run ahead of the other. Losing the Mantis had changed things. If they had stayed together in the first place, they would have stood a good chance of overwhelming the tengu. The lesson was clear; we are stronger together than alone.

They made their way down in a large, contiguous group in which there was neither leader nor sluggard. Whenever someone flagged, they waited together for them to catch their breath and whenever one of them tripped and fell at least two trainees would help them up. They had gone from being adversaries to being teammates. Undeniably, the many had become the sum of a whole.

All they had to do was return to the temple before sunset. Noke licked her teeth. *An easy enough task.*

Predictably, going down was far easier than climbing up. Within a few short hours, they had made work of their descent and some trainees were starting to whistle and sing as they got closer to the ground. They were sure of victory.

Noke stayed cautious. Too many times she had been lured by the sweet aroma of optimism, only to have joy snatched from her before she could taste it. She wasn't about to count her chickens yet. The test wasn't over.

They arrived at the village soon after and all seemed well. The streets were strangely quiet and that made Noke nervous again.

When at last they arrived at the Shugendo temple, the door was bolted shut. "Where is everyone?"

Minato stepped forward. "In the village temple," he said easily, "I heard the prayer call a few minutes ago."

Noke nodded her understanding. She had never been to the village temple before. Some of the other trainees had spoken about it, but she never had been interested.

"Let's go find them," Hiro said, hefting his sword over his shoulder.

They followed and at last came to the temple. A small man bowed at the door and asked them to take off their weapons.

"No weapons are allowed in the temple," the man said, "ever."

"Understood," Hiro said, dumping his swords into an unrolled carpet. "To spill blood in the temple is the highest abomination."

The others followed suit to drop their weapons on the carpet before they were allowed to step into the temple.

The main hall of the temple contained a large bathing chamber supported by four wooden columns. Its walls were decorated with red ochre paintings of beatific mountain scenes and six-petalled multifoil rosettes. A mural on the ceiling depicted the gods across a clear blue sky calling down to the world of humanity. At each corner of the chamber there were incense-burning thuribles and the floor was cut from polished oak.

"Remove you shoes," came a voice.

It was Tanto, unmistakable, even in a hall that large.

The other monks were there too - dressed in pure white kimono's and seated cross-legged on the floor. One monk stood at the center of the bath pool, up to the midriff in water. Only when Noke saw his face did she recognize who it was. It was only the second time Noke had seen Daishin, the Master Spiritual. A tall man, with almost faraway eyes.

Noke drew in a breath as she stepped into the room.

Kasa stepped forward and presented a clay bowl. "You were asked to bring leaves from the white tabunoki."

The trainees nodded and each dropped a leaf into the large clay bowl.

The Master Spiritual grinned. "Excellent, we will make a delicate tea this afternoon."

Noke arched an eyebrow. "Tea?"

The Master Spiritual nodded. "You should try it, very crisp and flavorful."

"We spent three days hungry, risking our lives! We lost the Mantis! We faced down a tengu! For you to make tea?!"

The Master Spiritual narrowed his eyes. "You," he said, studying her. He pinched her bicep. "You have come a long way, young lady. I am sorry that one of your number was lost – it is always a painful shame. But you need not blame his death on the unsuspecting tengu. There are many more common perils that can kill a young man in the mountains."

"There was a tengu," Noke insisted, "I saw it for myself."

Reshi nodded and raised his voice. "Kenji killed it."

The Master Spiritual's face grew hard as he turned on the boys. "You are being serious?"

Minato nodded his affirmation. "There was a strange fog Master, but some of us saw the tengu in the mist."

The Master Spiritual gave Kasa a glance for only a fraction of a moment before turning his gaze back to the trainees. "And which one of you is Kenji? Who slayed the tengu?"

Reshi pushed Kenji forward. Noke had only ever seen Kenji bullish or angry, but for the first time in her experience, Kenji seemed shy.

The Master Spiritual's jaw was tight as he spoke. "You killed the tengu?"

Kenji nodded awkwardly. "Yes, Master."

"How did you kill it?"

The Master Spiritual's stare was icy as death. Kenji looked away as he answered.

"I shot it with an arrow."

The Master Spiritual raised an eyebrow. "A single arrow?"

Kenji nodded. "Yes, Master."

The Master Spiritual glanced at Kasa, who also wore a hard look.

"Who else saw this tengu?" the Master Spiritual asked.

None of the others spoke. Noke swallowed hard. She wanted to keep everything about the tengu in a forgotten part of her mind, never to be remembered. Those dark eyes. That bird-beak nose. If she never spoke about a tengu again, it would still be too much.

The Master Spiritual asked again. "Who else saw it?"

Noke drew in a breath and stepped forward. "I did."

The Master Spiritual's eyes softened. "You? The girl."

Noke nodded. "My name is Nokemono."

He smiled. "What was it doing when you saw it?"

Noke cleared her throat. "It attacked me."

The Master Spiritual leaned forward. "Did you fight back?"

Noke hesitated. "Yes, I did."

"Then what happened?"

"I was sure it was going to kill me. It told me it already killed one of us and I saw the blood on its lips. Its kimono looked as though it had taken a bath in blood and its footsteps left a trail of red."

"You could understand its language?" the Master Spiritual asked.

Noke thought for a minute. Only then did she realize that the tengu had not spoken in any language she had heard before and yet, she understood it perfectly.

She nodded slowly. "Yes, I understood it."

"Why didn't it kill you?"

"I fought back. Just when I was sure it would strangle me to death a strange power came upon me and I felt the presence of a well of magic."

"Did you draw from it?" the Master Spiritual asked.

She nodded. "Yes, I did. It was…" she hesitated, "it was beautiful."

The Master Spiritual was silent for a long moment before he spoke again. "It was you, wasn't it? You killed the tengu."

Noke closed her eyes. "Yes, it was."

Reshi opened his mouth as though to process, but Minato put a hand over his mouth and whispered 'shut up'.

Noke was breathing hard. "What does it all mean?"

Master Spiritual said nothing for a long moment. The entire temple awaited his word. The tengu are creatures of another realm – they do not come here by chance or on a whim. If you truly saw a tengu, then it had a reason for revealing itself. Something it came to do."

"Something like what?"

The Master Spiritual looked up to the ceiling mural as though the gods depicted on it were to give him the answer. Then he sighed deeply and closed his eyes. "We cannot know. You are the only one who spoke to it, after all. You should have asked it why it came to earth?"

Noke frowned. "I was too busy trying to stop if from killing me to ask it questions."

The Master Spiritual's eyes opened again. "Well, whatever it came to do, I doubt it succeeded."

"Are the tengu a force for good or evil?" Noke asked.

In the spiritual realm, things are not so simple as that. There is no good. No evil. Everything is composed of both good and evil. The tengu are not evil, but they can also not be said to be good. They sometimes bring news of war. Sometimes they bring news of joy. Sometimes they are sent to disrupt the affairs of humanity."

"So it was trying to disrupt me," Noke said, "take me out of some grand picture?"

"Perhaps. Or maybe it came to your friend. The one that was killed. Though trainees have died on the test before, it is always a significant loss."

Noke nodded. "Of course, it must have been the Mantis. Why would I be of any importance at all?"

"We are all important in the grand picture," he turned to Noke, "But you child are specially important. You drew magic from a well unaided and were powerful enough to kill a tengu. That is no small feat. Even a well-trained Shugendo might have struggled with a full grown tengu. They are not easily defeated. I suspect that you are quite the important piece in the puzzle – the only question is, what part do you play in it? Are you of the darkness…or the light?"

"Do I not have any choice in the matter? Because I choose the light."

"We always have a choice, Nokemono. Always. I hope that when your great choices come, you make the right decisions. The choices we make are ripples in the great sea of life. Some ripples fizzle away, some become ocean waves that change everything."

Kasa stepped forward. "I have the feeling there are a few roaring waves in our cohort of trainees."

The Master Spiritual nodded. "What will be their next testing?"

"The tournament, Master," Kasa said, "from that, only five trainees will be admitted to the temple."

The Master Spiritual smiled. "Good luck to you all, then. May the best man," he hesitated, "or fighter, win."

Noke cleared her throat. "I have a question, Master."

The Master's eyebrows rose. "Go on."

"What if the tengus comes back?"

He narrowed his eyes. "What do you mean?"

"You said that the tengu are sent to earth to complete a specific task. If we have disrupted that task. What is to stop whoever sent it from sending more?"

"Nothing stops that, Nokemono."

"So, what do we do?"

The Master Spiritual's smile widened. "We prepare and when the time comes, we make a choice. May our choices becalm the sea."

CHAPTER TWENTY

The days before the tournament were the hardest of all. Losing the Mantis had changed the mood of the entire cohort of trainees. Now everyone joined the early morning training and that meant the sparring was harder and more competitive. No one took it easy, every worked hard. There were no weak links.

It meant that working in the day wasn't enough. Noke took to working at night too. After practicing the forms with Sora. She would have her dinner and go for a private run around the village with a bag loaded with uncooked rice she borrowed from the kitchen. Her body, once of soft clay, had become a thing of stone. When she punched, she got a reaction, even from Hiro. When she checked a kick, she heard the sound of bone on bone. She gave it her all, knowing that when the tournament came, she would not fail for want of trying. Noke would leave the Shugendo temple only as a corpse or a captive. She would not be leaving a failure.

On tournament day, the bell rang earlier than usual. Noke was already awake and had worked herself into a slight sweat from her morning stretches. She met Sora and Minato out in the corridor, and they both looked a little nervous.

"Today is the day," Sora announced, his voice cracking a little as he spoke.

Noke only nodded in response. She felt far away from them in that moment. If the draw was unkind, she would have to face one of her two friends in the tournament; she didn't want happy memories in her head if she had to beat one of them until they couldn't stand.

"I'm eating breakfast alone today," she said, without a hint of warmth in her voice. "I hope you understand."

Sora's eyes widened, but Minato gave an affirming nod. "I understand."

Breakfast was heartier than usual and that was saying something for the Shugendo temple. If rumor was to be believed, there had been times when trainees had died in the final tournament. It made sense then for a prospective last meal to be a memorable one.

She saw Hiro walk past with his shoulders hunched and eyes narrowed to slits. He was always friendly in the dining hall, but today he looked like he was already in a fight. Everyone knew what was coming.

When the time for the tournament arrived, all the trainees were early to the fighting circle. They had their wooden swords at hand and only made eye contact where absolutely necessary. The tension was thick as a cinder brick.

Kasa and Tanto arrived uncommonly late. It was as though they wanted the tension to reach its fullness before their grand entrance. As they stepped inside the room, there was an almost palpable release of a collectively held breathes. As the trainees transitioned from thinking about an uncertain future to living in the crunching now.

"Welcome," Kasa began. "We all know why we are here. To test your fighting spirits. I want you to know that those who are admitted into the Shugendo after this tournament will not be selected purely on their number of wins here. There are ten times a hundred ways to fight without ever lifting a sword, a fist or even a voice. We are here to see who has understood, most spectacularly, the essence of the Shugendo. Patience, diligence, resilience and concentration. These were the things I asked you to learn when we first began. Now show us what you have learned. Ten thousand push-ups."

There moment when they all looked at each other. It had been so long since they had been asked to do push-ups that the response was delayed.

Minato did the mathematics and called out the number. "Seven hundred and seventy."

Noke was the first to drop to her knees. Minato followed suit and soon they were all doing push-ups in perfect unison. It was beyond Noke's comprehension. How Kasa expected them to fight following the exhaustion caused by the numerous push-ups they had completed. Her only focus was to reach seven hundred and seventy push-ups.

Hiro finished first, but stayed with his palms down in case he needed to make up for anyone else. He wasn't needed. Everyone finished their full complement of push-ups. Seven hundred and seventy each.

It felt as though someone had taken a hammer and pounded her arms into a watery pulp. The thought of having to pick a sword up and defend herself seemed unthinkable.

"Resilience," Kasa announced. "You are all tired, all fatigued. Can you carry on? Let's find out. Swords up."

Tanto brought out his bucket of swords and started passing them around. Noke's arm sagged as she hefted the sword. She was in pain and a little tired, but with a sword in her hand, wooden or otherwise, she was no easy prey. Whoever she faced in the circle would meet a challenge.

Minato's name was the first called. He was faced off against Reshi, who seemed the less enthused by the match. Kasa gave the call to start, and Minato closed the distance in two quick strides. What followed was a decimation that was so brutally comprehensive that it made the complete circle go quiet. Usually the trainees shouted out their favorites as a bout went on but the cold, merciless way that Minato destroyed Reshi left everyone stunned to total silence. The only sound was that of sword against bone, as Minato made quick work of his helpless opponent. When Reshi tried to open the fight, with 'monkey climbs the tree.' Minato feinted with 'rushing wave' and shifted quickly into 'Tiger strikes.' It was an effortless change of style so deft and sharp that it caught everyone by surprise. Once Minato got inside Reshi's reach, it was over. He lashed out with the sword and didn't stop until Reshi screamed his surrender.

When the bout was over, everyone stared in silence for a long moment as Tanto made sure that Reshi was still alive.

When Reshi raised a hand, Tanto let out a sigh of relief.

Kasa smiled. "And so, it begins."

Aki beat a skinny trainee they called Ken, while Sora won a close bout with Hyu. Hiro would have been just as impressive as Minato in his breaking of Jin, but the smaller trainee was so quick to surrender that Hiro barely got a chance to uncoil.

To no one's surprise, Nokemono was paired up against Kenji.

The two had fought more times than anyone else and had a deep and private enmity that ran deeper than bone marrow. Kenji had won far more fights, but in the recent sessions it was plain that Nokemono was becoming a dangerous competition. More than once she had managed to beat him in close-fought fights.

Noke wondered as she stepped into the circle if Kenji had been holding back in the same way Minato did. If he had a sudden quickness that he had hidden from everyone until he first meant to use it. She doubted that highly. Kenji was about as subtle as a street sign. There was nothing complex or hidden about him – he was just a tall, musclebound lout with a bigger mouth than a brain. *No surprises there.*

That thought lingered in Noke's mind as she considered her strategy. *No surprises.* She rubbed her chin as the whisper of a plan started forming in her head.

Kenji was a blissfully simple fighter. He was competent with the forms and very skilled at defending himself, but his weapon of choice was his spite. When it came to making a fight dirty – he was a master. But Noke had grown up fighting the rats for scraps of food. She could fight with the dirtiest of them. She could scratch with every punch and turn the sword just enough to nick the nose with every swipe. It meant their fights always wore each other out. She knew what Kenji expected of her – a fight dirty to the elbow. A more intense scrap than all their fights before. She wasn't going to give that to him.

If Kenji was expecting a street fight, then she would take him to the emperor's quadrangle. She would fight a fight so numbingly clean that he would lose all parts of his game plan. He was the better trained, of that there was no doubt. He had studied the forms for years before Noke even knew what a form was, but she had the advantage of ingenuity. She had seen things that a temple boy like Kenji never would have. A fisherman drawing in the catch, a meat cooker swatting away the flies, a pickpocket stealing a bracelet from a man's still-shaking hand. There was artistry in all those things, too. Rhythm and Noke had learned to ally pieces of that to what she knew of the Shugendo.

"Fight!" Kasa announced.

The word almost took her by surprise. She was so deep into her plan that she had forgotten that now was the time to enact it. Kenji charged at her and only a clutch of practice-won instinct allowed her to bring her sword up in time. She anticipated his uppercut and brushed it aside as she scrambled out of rage. Then she feinted as though going for his throat stone. He took the bait like a hungry fish and hopped back, holding the sword up. Noke smiled. She wasn't going for his throat; she was going for his calf – as classic a target area as was to be found in the Shugendo. Kasa had once told them that calf kicks were the bread and milk of their fighting diet – Noke was set for a feast. She struck hard, fast, and merciless. Kenji buckled and let out a broken cry as he raised his sword. Noke brought her sword down in the space between neck and shoulder and kicked him in the chest. He went down with a wheeze of blown out breath. Noke could have hurt him. She could have thumped him with a headshot so hard it would shatter his teeth. But somehow, she knew this was not the time. She put her sword to his chest. "Do you yield?"

He looked up at her, his eyes glinting with the promise of tears and let out a loud, resigned breath.

"Say it," Noke insisted. "Say it or I end it myself."

He closed his eyes and raised his chin. "I yield."

The crowd exploded. Noke glanced over her shoulder in surprise as she noticed what all the cheering was about. It was her name. They were cheering for her.

"Noke! Noke! Noke!"

She closed her eyes, feeling the tears touch the top of her cheeks. Thirteen fighters had become six. That meant she only needed to win one more fight to qualify as one of the finest five.

She leaned down to her beaten foe and whispered something he had once whispered to her. "Time's up."

He narrowed his eyes and Noke saw that he was touched with incandescent rage. That made her smile a little.

Kasa raised her hand. "Victory to Nokemono."

She covered her mouth, astounded by the sound of applause. Then the excitement cut off as she realized why they were really cheering. Across the circle stood Hiro tilting his neck one way, then the other.

Kasa pointed. "Your next opponent, Hiro."

Noke's heart fell. *That is why they were cheering. They knew I would be facing Hiro next.*

Noke drew in a silent breath and closed her eyes. "They want me to die."

Minato's hand fell upon her shoulder. "Don't worry, he likes you. He'll give you a chance to surrender without shame."

Noke felt her stomach drop. *Surrender without shame.* That was not why she had come here. Not why she fought. Shame is the bane of those who have not had the pleasure of eating with pigs from the trough. It wasn't shame that brought her here; it was the Kazeshini and being a Shugendo was the only way she was going to take it. *I can't lose.*

Kasa raised both hands to applaud. "Congratulations all. You have made it through the first day. You have proven your resilience. Tomorrow, the fight continues."

Noke frowned, unsurprised by the announcement. Fighting a well-rested Hiro seemed far more dangerous than fighting him now, but she had no choice. If beating Hiro was the only way to become one of the Shugendo, then it was what she had to do. *Corpse or a captive. The only way I leave this temple.*

When the fighting was done for the day, she wandered out into the village in search of a reprieve. She had only been walking a while when she had that feeling again. A calling, a demanding. Something reaching out to her.

Her first instinct was to turn towards the sword, but this call came from another direction. She glanced over her shoulder. *The village temple.*

She sauntered towards the temple as the feeling swelled in her stomach. The calling was clear as the town crier's plea.

"Drop your weapons," said the man at the door.

Noke glanced down at the sword she carried. Since the test of the mountains, she had kept it at her side. She dropped it on the carpet, removed her shoes and stepped inside.

The Master Spiritual sat alone beside the water. The smell of incense was thick in the air and it seemed as though all the noise from outside the temple had been cut off completely – there was total silence.

He glanced over his shoulder and met her gaze. His eyes were still and expressionless as the night sea, and he had an aura that Noke could only interpret as pride. You didn't need to see the weapons to know that he was a man of power. There was something unmistakable in his manner and bearing.

He sniffed at the air as though catching the whiff of something.

Noke could smell it too. Smoke. Something big was burning.

The Master Spiritual narrowed his eyes.

A voice sounded behind Nokemono and she nearly jumped out of her skin.

"Wonderful," came the raspy, twisted voice.

The word was spoken in a language she had only ever heard once. A language she could not be sure how she understood. The language of the tengu.

The Master Spiritual lowered his eyes and gestured to Nokemono. Get behind me.

Without turning back, she obeyed and stepped into his shadow. Only then did she see what she had feared to look at.

Eye's pinkish white, nose beakish long, teeth dripping with blood. *Another tengu.*

The creature smiled a terrible smile and blood leaked down the side of its mouth. "This time, there will be no escape."

EPILOGUE

Nokemono reached immediately for her sword but felt nothing but the cloth of her kimono. Her weapons were outside, past the tengu.

Each heartbeat hit like a punch against her chest. Her breath came in brief gasps. She balled her hands up into fists and crouched low. *Corpse or a captive.*

The temple was supposed to be a meeting place with the gods. It didn't feel like the gods were near now. How could a creature such as this enter this holy place?

The Master Spiritual rose slowly to his feet. There was a sureness to him. A confidence unlike most that Noke had seen.

The creature took four steps towards them and yet, with every step it took, the calmer the Master Spiritual appeared to become. The man was a master to fear. Noke wondered if anything in the world could make a man like him afraid. He looked upon the tengu as though it was an old forgotten shoe, or a leaf fall astray from its tree. Completely indifferent.

The Master Spiritual cleared his throat, raised his chin and spoke in the tengu language. His voice was as deep and vast as the ocean. "Why have you come here tengu?"

Noke understood it with the casual ease of a native speaker. Somehow, this strange language was not new to her.

The tengu bared its teeth. "I have come for the girl."

The Master Spiritual did not seem surprised. He raised his right hand across his chest and folded the other one behind his back. "You cannot have her."

The tengu raised an eyebrow. "Who are you?"

The Master Spiritual straightened. "I am Daishin. The Master Spiritual of the Shugendo temple."

The tengu hissed and made a coughing sound. "I have heard of you. You are a monk. No stranger to the work of the higher world."

The Master Spiritual nodded once. "So, you know my work."

Somehow, Daishin was utterly calm. He spoke to the tengu as though he was an trainee. Even this nightmare was no cause for terror to him.

The tengu narrowed its eyes. "I have no quarrel with you, Daishin." The creature raised a gnarled claw and held it out. One finger bore a single gold ring. "Do you know who I am?" the tengu asked.

The Master Spiritual's voice was devoid of emotion. "You are Cenku. Lord of tengu. Servant of the light and dark."

"So, you know my work?"
The Master Spiritual nodded again. "Intimately."

The two stood for a moment, weighing each other up. The world seemed to stand still for that moment. Silence before the storm.

Just then, someone burst into the room with a flash of steel and sand. It was Ikeda Cen, the Master Spiritual's acolyte. He held a weapon pointed directed at the tengu - a long, curved blade with a golden ornamented hilt.

The tengu bared its teeth again and raised its hand. Talons sprouted from its gnarled claws as it made a hissing sound, hunched for attack.

"This is a temple," the Master Spiritual shouted. "There will be no blood spilled on holy ground."

The creature lowered his neck but did not drop its talons. Ikeda Cen did not lower his sword.

The Master Spiritual spoke again. "We do not bring weapons upon holy ground."

Ikeda Cen's eyes bulged as he aimed his sword at the tengu. "Master, the demon has no respect for our custom."

The Master Spiritual raised a hand, gentle as the night breeze. "That is what makes us different from the demons, Ikeda Cen. What makes us better than them? We are light in the darkness. We do not bend our laws for anyone. Drop your weapon."

Ikeda Cen gave the Master a long, bewildered look. "Master."

The Master Spiritual narrowed his eyes. "Drop it."

Slowly, reluctantly, Ikeda Cen dropped his weapon.

The Master Spiritual gave the tengu a look and it let out a breath, pulling its claws back and straightening to civility.

The Master Spiritual spoke again in the tengu language. "I see we find ourselves at something of an impasse."

The tengu nodded. "So I will offer you a deal."

The Master Spiritual nodded. "Speak it."

"I can take the girl and trouble you no more," the tengu shot Noke a studying look and as it's red-rimmed eyes passed over her, she felt a sickening tremor of fear, "or I can take you and the girl will be spared."

"And my acolyte?" the Master Spiritual asked.

"He will be spared as well." The tengu will trouble this village no more.

There was silence for a long moment as the tengu awaited the Master Spiritual's response.

The Master Spiritual grinned. "You give me a simple choice, demon. I would happily give my life a thousand times, for anyone innocent of my temple."

"No, Master!" Ikeda Cen screamed.

Daishin raised a hand. "It is my choice, Ikeda. Surely you do not mean to deny me my own choice."

Ikeda Cen was silenced, his head slumping forward like a sulking child.

The tengu closed its eyes and for a moment, it didn't look like a demon at all. It was as though – for that one eternal moment – it had stepped into the light and become something else. Something better.

"You are an honorable man, Daishin, and one amongst ten thousand."

They clasped hands, tengu and man, sealing their solemn agreement.

Noke looked up to the Master Spiritual and breathed a single word. "Why?"

The Master Spiritual smiled. "Because you are more than you know you are Nokemono. I knew it from when I was first told what you said to Tanto, when you first tried to steal the Wind of Death."

Noke gave him a sharp look. "What did I say?"

He smiled. "Even the wolf who howls at the moon can still be brought again to light. That is the work of the temple. To be a light in the darkness. A place of restoration. Of sanctuary. Of redemption."

Ikeda Cen sank to his knees. "Let the demon take me Master, I will go, please."

The tengu snorted and muttered something in its sharp tongue.

The Master Spiritual raised a hand. "This is my sacrifice and mine alone, Ikeda. You will be the Master Spiritual now." He turned to Noke, took her hand and folded something in it, closing her fist tight. It was a key.

She glanced up at him. "For what?"

He leaned close. "You will know when the time comes," the Master Spiritual whispered. "Reveal it to no one."

A stiff wind blew through the temple and the tengu snorted out a hot breath. "It is time, Master Daishin."

Daishin nodded, smiled one last time and walked as a king would out from the temple and into the fog with the tengu.

Ikeda Cen let out a horrified scream and charged after them with his weapon. Nokemono didn't need to look to know the new Master Spiritual would not catch them. By the time he got outside, they would be gone.

She stared down at the key and saw words inscribed along the teeth. *The Shugendo Key. Patience, diligence, resilience and concentration.*

www.ingramcontent.com/pod-product-compliance
Lightning Source LLC
Chambersburg PA
CBHW060700190726
48289CB00002B/486